➤ **WESLEY ELLIS** ◆

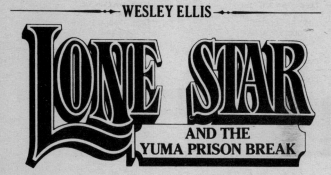

LONE STAR

AND THE YUMA PRISON BREAK

JOVE BOOKS, NEW YORK

LONE STAR AND THE YUMA PRISON BREAK

A Jove Book / published by arrangement with
the author

PRINTING HISTORY
Jove edition / September 1991

ISBN: 0-515-10670-4

Jove Books are published by The Berkley Publishing Group,
200 Madison Avenue, New York, New York 10016.
The name "JOVE" and the "J" logo
are trademarks belonging to Jove Publications, Inc.

PRINTED IN THE UNITED STATES OF AMERICA

10   9   8   7   6   5   4   3   2   1

JAILHOUSE BRAWL

"All right," a deep voice growled. "I guess it's yellow-ass kicking time." Big Al was ape-like, with a lantern jaw, a thick overhang of brow, and a low forehead. His arms were too long for his body, and his legs were short, but thick as barrels. Al stepped inside the cell. "What are you in for?"

"Assault," Ki answered.

"You whipped a man?" Al asked, his voice dripping with contempt. "A damn runty little Chinaman."

"I'm a samurai."

"You're meat," Al growled, advancing with his fingers splayed wide.

Ki set his feet on the hard-packed cell floor. Most men would ball their fists and come at you—this one had no intention of administering a beating—he was out to break his opponent's neck or throttle him to death. . . .

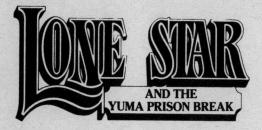

LONE STAR

AND THE
YUMA PRISON BREAK

★

Chapter 1

The tall cattle rancher from San Antonio reined his horse up beside Jessie's palomino and dismounted. He had been struggling all afternoon to take his eyes off Jessie as they'd ridden her huge Circle Star Ranch, looking at cattle he was in the market to buy. Now, he finally studied the thousand or so Longhorn cows and knew he was looking at quality beef.

"They're as fine a breeding herd as I've ever seen," he said, tying his horse beside the palomino and walking out to stand beside Jessie. "How'd you get such quality?"

"I breed for size and conformation," Jessie explained. "When my father first came to Texas, everyone said that the Texas Longhorns could run like deer and fight like cougars but they tasted and chewed like rawhide. Right from the start, my father and I started breeding for quality instead of quantity. I've had buyers tell me over and over that Circle Star beef earns them extra dollars at the market. We try and cull out the cows that are long and stringy looking. I want cattle that carry muscle with a little fat for flavoring."

1

"Jessie, it sounds to me like you've got some pretty radical ideas, then," Orin Clark said. "Most Texas ranchers are interested in cattle that multiply and can sprint like rabbits."

Jessie laughed outright. She and Orin Clark had been dealing in cattle for the past three years. His only problem, as far as she could tell, was that he seemed to have a difficult time concentrating on cows instead of her figure.

"How many are you looking to buy this year?"

"Depends on the price."

"Thirty-five dollars a head if you take the herd, forty a head if you cream them for the best."

Orin whistled softly. "Why that's five, maybe seven dollars above the market."

"Sure it is," Jessie said. "You'll pay a little more for quality no matter if you're buying horses, cattle, or any other thing."

Orin frowned. He knew Jessie was right. He could not find a herd of mother cows of this quality if he spent a year and covered every cattle ranch in the whole darned Southwest.

"I do like them," he said. "Mostly three and four year olds?"

"Yes," she said. "They've had one calf last spring."

"Percentage?"

"About seventy percent."

Orin clucked with appreciation. Out on the range, if you got a seventy percent calf crop, you were doing exceptionally well. "I can see that most of them are bred right now."

"That's right," Jessie told him. "I keep a range bull out here for every hundred cows. They've all been bred more than once."

2

Even as they watched, a big brindle bull trotted after a cow, chasing her toward them. Normally, it was dangerous to be afoot with a Longhorn bull but not when the animal's huge penis was stiff and flopping between his legs and his mind was strictly on riding a cow in heat.

"Get her," Orin said, forgetting himself for a moment because a bred cow was money in a cattleman's pockets. "Get her!"

The bull didn't need urging. It was a huge beast, nearly twice the size of the young sand-colored cow, and when it dangled its muscular forelegs down the cow's back and its arm-length penis bounced up and found the cow's swollen and ready vagina, the bull did not waste time with preliminaries.

The cow lowed loudly as the bull rammed almost a yard of its meat into her and then began to hunch its great body into the much smaller animal.

Jessie felt her cheeks warm a little as she glanced sideways at Orin. He was grinning as the bull had its brutish way with the small cow, and she thought she saw a little envy in his eyes.

It did not last long. Less than a minute until the bull, with a deep groan, emptied himself into the cow and then climbed off of her, penis swinging like the pendulum of a big clock.

"That's a good breeding bull," Orin said, turning to Jessie and looking deep into her eyes. "I can see that that little cow is going to calve. And if you'll notice, she didn't try to run away very hard."

"She knew it was of no use," Jessie said. "She knew that bull would track her down even if she ran five miles."

Orin's mouth was dry with desire. He licked his lips and stepped up to Jessie. In a thick voice, he said, "This is the

3

third year that I've been coming out here and buying your cows, and for some reason, I always feel the same way when I see them breed and I'm standing beside you."

"What way?"

He reached out and touched her cheek, his heart pounding. "I watch my own bulls breed my own cows a thousand times a year and I don't feel anything. But here with you, it's about to drive me crazy. I expect you know why."

"Sure. You want me to be a cow and you'll be my bull. Isn't that it?"

He managed to nod. "That's it. I want to chase you down and mount you, Jessie. I can't help it that you put a fever in my blood whenever we're together."

Jessie reached out and unbuttoned the top button on his shirt. "Thirty-five dollars a head," she whispered, drawing him up to her. "Cash on the barrel."

"You gonna throw in a free breeding?"

"You just saw it," she teased.

"That's not the one that I want," he said, his big hands reaching around to cup her behind, clad in tight denim pants.

Jessie laughed softly. "I don't usually throw myself into a deal," she told him, "but I can see that you are in real need of some satisfaction."

"I sure am," he said as she unbuttoned his shirt and then began to kiss his nipples so that he thought he was going to bust out of his own britches.

A moment later, they were on the grass, rolling and laughing, tearing each other's clothes off, Orin mounting Jessie with all the vigor of a Longhorn bull.

"Yes," she panted, grabbing his buttocks and pulling him into her, feeling his huge, throbbing manhood plunging in and out.

4

Orin's eyes glazed with pleasure and he completely abandoned all reserve as their bodies thrust faster and faster at each other, until they were both crying out with pleasure and he filled Jessie with his seed.

"Dear beautiful woman," he breathed, "you are everything I expected and more!"

Jessie looked up into his eyes. "This is a hell of a poor way of doing business, you know."

He laughed and kissed her, then rolled off to lie staring up at the flat blue sky. "I guess that, from now on, you can ask about any price you want and I'll have to pay it. Was that your thinking, Jessie?"

"No," she said. "It's just that each of the past two years you've come, I knew that you left this ranch in such a heat that you could hardly think straight. I just figured that, sooner or later, you had to be serviced or you'd forget why you came to my ranch."

He laughed. "I didn't know my need for you was so obvious."

"It was. I could have sold you antelope, and I don't think you'd have objected or maybe known the difference until you got back to San Antonio."

"There's truth in that," he admitted. "I'd be thinking about nothing but you for a month before I got here and for a month after. I've even dreamed that . . ."

"What?"

"Well, that maybe you might even be talked into selling out here and coming over toward San Antonio. It's prettier country."

"Uh-uh," Jessie said. "I like this part of West Texas just fine. It's a little drier and hotter, maybe not as green, but this is where my father sank his roots and Circle Star is now too much a part of me to ever leave."

5

"I was afraid of that. I guess there's too much of your father here, huh?"

Jessie nodded. "He was an empire builder. He owned companies around the world, but this ranch owned his heart. He was happier here than anywhere else on earth. I am, too."

Orin nodded. "It's a beautiful spread, all right. It's so big it makes mine look like small potatoes."

"There's nothing small about thirty thousand acres, Orin. You're one of the best and most successful ranchers in Texas."

"And I'd be even more successful if we could . . ."

Jessie placed a finger across his lips. "I'll look forward to your cattle-buying visit every spring, but our lives are too complicated to blend. Let's just enjoy what little time we have together."

Orin took her into his arms and laid her back down on the grass. "I might be tempted to buy so many cattle from you that I'll overstock my range."

"I don't think so," Jessie said as she kissed his mouth. "But if you do run out of land, I might even lease you a few thousand acres of Circle Star."

"My oh my," he said, gently pushing Jessie's silken thighs apart, "you are *such* a pleasure to deal with!"

It was late that afternoon when Jessie and Orin Clark approached Circle Star headquarters, where Ki, her samurai, and Ed Wright, her longtime foreman, anxiously waited.

"Something is wrong," Jessie said the moment she saw the pair standing in the ranch yard waiting for her.

"Maybe there's good news of some kind."

"No," Jessie told him. "Good news can always wait, bad news never will."

6

When they galloped into the yard and dismounted, Jessie and Orin handed their reins over to a ranch hand and Jessie took one glance at her foreman and samurai, then said, "What happened?"

Ed Wright handed her a letter. "It's old Judge Stanley Appleton. He was murdered, and this letter came from his daughter. Pearl says that she is under a death threat."

Jessie took the letter and read it quickly. There was not much more to learn than what her foreman had already told her. But reading the letter, Jessie was struck by the desperation in Pearl's words and the fact that several other judges had been murdered or had received death threats.

"It doesn't sound like they have any idea who is doing this," the samurai said. "Do you want me to go and help her?"

"I think we'd both better go," Jessie said. "One of us might have to watch Pearl while the other tries to discover what is going on back there."

"I could come if you need me," Orin said.

"No," Jessie said quickly, "but thank you. We'll ride hard and fast and perhaps even bring Pearl back with us for safekeeping."

"How old would she be now?" Orin asked. "I haven't seen her or the judge in at least five years."

"Pearl would be about nineteen or twenty," Jessie said. "And the last time I saw her, she had the promise of being a beauty."

"A badly frightened young beauty," Ki said, his face grim. "You can read between the lines and almost feel the heartache and the terror."

Jessie nodded. "She doesn't say how her father was murdered or any of the circumstances. I wish we were a lot closer to Tucson. It will be a hard journey."

7

"When will you be leaving?" Ed asked.

"Tomorrow at daybreak," Jessie replied.

The men exchanged silent glances and said nothing as Jessie walked into the house and went to her office, where she sat down at a huge rolltop desk that had once belonged to her father.

Jessie rolled up the desk and withdrew a piece of stationery. She would draw up a bill of sale for the one thousand cattle that Orin had agreed to buy. Then, she would spend three or four hours catching up on paperwork that had to be attended to before her departure.

"Miss Jessie?"

Jessie turned to see her housekeeper and friend, Emma, standing in the doorway. The old woman was normally smiling, but now she had a worried look on her face. "Miss Jessie, can I bring you some food? I got a nice roast and plenty of. . . ."

"No, thank you," Jessie said, "I'm not hungry."

"I heard that you and Mr. Ki will be leaving at dawn. I sure do wish you'd eat something tonight. It'd make you stronger for tomorrow."

But Jessie shook her head. "Please give this bill of sale to Mr. Clark along with my apologies."

"He won't accept no apologies, Miss Jessie. But I'll give him the bill of sale. I sure am sad about Judge Appleton. He was about the best friend your father ever had."

"I know that," Jessie said. "When my father was just starting to build his import/export business in San Francisco, it was Stan Appleton who took him on as a client and kept him from making a few critical legal mistakes that would have set him back in business. And years later, when Stan became a judge, I remember how proud my father was of him."

Emma nodded. "Can I at least bring you some coffee and cookies?"

"All right," Jessie said, knowing there was no sense in upsetting her dear housekeeper, who would take a good deal of comfort in serving her.

When Emma left, Jessie turned back to her paperwork. She had been remiss in letting some of it slip a little behind. Now, there were matters to settle regarding both her rubber plantation in South America and her coffee plantation in Brazil. From the southern part of Africa, there were matters of some urgency regarding her diamond mine and from London, England, a question regarding the possible acquisition of a shipbuilding yard.

Jessie sighed. Her father had been assassinated by an international cartel whose aim had been nothing less than domination of the world banking system. Had her father yielded to the cartel, he would still be alive and richer than ever. But Alex Starbuck had not resisted. Instead, he'd fought the cartel and almost succeeded in its destruction before he was gunned down.

Jessie had been in her teens then and had had to take on an enormous amount of responsibility for her age. But she'd done it and done it well enough that the Starbuck empire was, if anything, bigger and in better financial health than ever before. And that's the way she intended it to remain. It was her father's legacy, and she would protect his holdings and his friends just as ferociously as he would have protected them.

It was simply a matter of honor.

★

Chapter 2

At the first light of dawn, Jessie and Ki walked out to the barn and their saddled and waiting horses. Ki was carrying his traditional samurai bow and quiver of arrows, and Jessie was wearing a Colt strapped to her shapely hip and a Winchester in a well-worn rifle boot.

Ed Wright had personally made sure that all of their traveling supplies were packed into their saddlebags and that their saddles, bridles, and other gear were cleaned and well oiled. Jessie's palominio, Sun, had had worn shoes, and so the animal had been freshly shod. Ki's pinto had been brushed to a shine.

"I always worry about you going across Apache country," Ed told them. "Geronimo might be on the warpath again someplace. He keeps bustin' out of the San Carlos Indian Reservation and raising hell."

"We'll keep an eye out for him," Jessie promised. "And neither Ki nor myself is ashamed to run. I've never seen Indian ponies that are the match of our horses."

"Me neither," the Circle Star foreman admitted, "but any

horse can come up lame—even these two."

"You worry too much," the samurai said.

"I get paid to worry. I worry about cattle, feed, water, the price of beef at the railhead in Abilene, Kansas, and the weather. And I worry about you and Apaches, not to mention whatever the deuce kind of trouble you're heading for over in Tucson."

Jessie patted her foreman on the arm. Since her father had died, Ed Wright had assumed a special place in her heart, and she knew he considered her his adopted daughter.

Jessie mounted her horse and Ki did the same, and just as they were about to ride out, Orin Clark appeared. He looked sheepish. "I meant to awaken hours ago and help Ed give you a send-off, but I overslept."

"Go back to bed," Jessie said with a smile. "You'll have darn little rest until you get the cows you bought over to your range."

"Thanks for the bill of sale," Orin said. "I'll be back again about this time next year. And I know a few folks in Tucson, so if you need some people you can trust. . . ."

"We'll be fine," Jessie said. "I've got a few acquaintances there myself. The main thing is just to get there and find out who murdered the judge and then make sure that Pearl's life isn't in any danger."

Orin nodded and stepped back. He looked as if he wanted to say something personal to Jessie, but since this was not the time or the place, she touched spurs to her horse and Sun responded by moving into a easy gallop that took her across the yard and up the road leading west toward Arizona.

The samurai stayed right behind, his eyes already watchful of everything. Unlike Jessie, who had ridden horses since her earliest childhood, Ki was not an expert horseman. In fact, he preferred to walk rather than ride. Ki submitted to horseback riding because he knew that he could not keep up with Jessie on foot, although he was in such splendid physical condition that he could run effortlessly for many miles.

It took Jessie and Ki three days of hard riding to reach El Paso. When they arrived, the main topic of conversation was another fierce Apache leader, Tatona.

"He's a distant cousin of Geronimo," Sheriff Wes Hillard told them. "And from what I hear, he's vicious. Leads a band of about thirty warriors and he don't give a damn who he murders."

Ki glanced sideways at Jessie. "We could wait for the next stage and board our horses here."

"I don't think you like that idea any more than I do," Jessie said.

But the sheriff disagreed. "Listen, the stageline stopped running two weeks ago, but there's going to be a special stage leaving tomorrow morning under heavy guard. And I mean *real* heavy. I hear the company has more than thirty thousand dollars in cash, gold, and silver that they have to deliver to the army in Tucson. So my advice would be to go with them."

"They may be filled."

"Not for you and Ki they won't be," the sheriff said. "If you want, I'll personally talk to the stageline officials. Even if the coach is full, you could still ride alongside and have the comfort of numbers working for you and against the Apache."

Jessie frowned. She had Ki had always had the best luck traveling unencumbered by others. However, if this Tatano and his band of warriors were out there raising hell, then it might be wise to have some company. Jessie remembered her foreman's words about how any horse could go lame.

12

And if that happened between El Paso and Tucson, they'd be in a terrible fix.

"Go ahead and talk to them," Jessie said. "Tell the stage officials that we will certainly pay the regular fare."

"Hell no!" Hillard exclaimed. "It's you and Ki that ought to be paid, not the other way around."

"Whatever," Jessie said.

That night, they ate well at an excellent steak house named Clyde's Cow Palace, and when they were about to leave, Sheriff Hillard appeared. "I had some trouble talking the stageline into allowing you to join them. They're worried about lawsuits in the event they were attacked and something happened to either one of you that was beyond their control."

"Then we'll just go our own way," Jessie said.

"No, no, you don't need to do that. The man in charge is named Frank Ranger, and he's agreed to let you, Jessie, ride inside the coach. But I'm afraid that your friend is going to have to either ride on the roof or his horse."

Jessie was incensed. "If Ki isn't welcome in the coach, then neither am I."

The sheriff sighed. "Listen, Jessie, I know that Frank can be a little difficult and unreasonable, but he knows his business and he'll be a damn good man to have on your side if there's trouble. And besides Frank, there will be five other men with rifles guarding that coach, and you can bet that every last one will be a marksman."

"I still say I won't ride inside."

"Jessie," Ki said, "I would prefer to ride on the roof of the coach anyway. It is not important."

"It is to me."

Sheriff Hillard frowned. "Listen, it's not that late. Why don't we just walk over to the stageline and see if the three of you can work out the details? The main thing is, you need to stick together out there. Even with all the firepower you'll have, you'd still be mighty shorthanded against Tatano and thirty of his veteran fighters."

"All right," Jessie said, "let's go on over and speak to this man. But I'm sure not pleased about his insistence that Ki can't be seated in the coach."

A few minutes later, Ki and Jessie, escorted by the sheriff, arrived at the offices of the El Paso Stage Company. It was dark and the office was locked, but there was a light on inside and they could hear voices.

"Who is it?" a rough voice demanded.

"Sheriff Hillard. I got Miss Starbuck and her friend, Ki, with me. We need to talk to Frank. Open up."

They heard a key in the door scratch the lock before it opened to reveal no less than six hard-looking men inside, seated around a table playing cards and drinking whiskey.

"Frank," the sheriff said, motioning Jessie forward, "this is Miss Starbuck."

Frank Ranger was a short, barrel-chested man in his early thirties. He had a fist-busted nose, a lantern jaw, and deep-set black eyes under a heavy bridge of bone. Those eyes seemed to bore right through Jessie and Ki as they crossed the room.

Jessie extended her hand. "I understand that we have a little difference of opinion as to where Ki will be seated," Jessie said, coming right to the issue without any of the usual small talk.

"Difference of opinion?" Ranger said, his thick eyebrows lifting in question as he tore his eyes from Jessie to regard Ki with unconcealed dislike. "There's no difference of opinion that I can see. The company policy is that we don't allow Indians, Nigras, or Chinamen to ride in our coaches.

14

They ride on top—or they don't ride at all."

"That's what I thought this was all about," Jessie said, her eyes flashing with anger. "And for the record, your company policy stinks to high heaven."

Ranger's cheeks colored with anger. "Lady, I've heard all about you. You're so damn rich and powerful that you think you can just run roughshod over everyone, that you can buy or sell people or companies at your pleasure. Well, the truth of the matter is that I ain't for sale and neither is my company."

"I'm not interested in either at any price," Jessie said, starting to turn around.

Frank Ranger, stung by Jessie's dismissal, grabbed her by the arm, and his fingers bit into Jessie's flesh. She winced and tried to wrench free, but Ranger held on tight until the iron-hard edge of the samurai's hand chopped down against the base of his skull, dropping him to his knees.

The other stageline employees jumped out of their seats, and they would have attacked Ki except that the sheriff and Jessie both had already drawn and aimed their Colts.

"Sit down, all of you!" the sheriff raged. "What the hell is the matter with you people! You're going across a country overrun with Apache, and you need all the help you can get. And here you are fighting amongst yourselves."

"Save it, Sheriff," Jessie said, looking down at the dazed stageline owner. "I wouldn't ride with a man like that if he paid me."

"Now hang on a minute!" The sheriff swore.

But Jessie wasn't listening. She had seen men like Frank Ranger before, and they were brutish, insensitive, and usually stupid. A man like that would be a liability rather than an asset in times of trouble.

"We'll be leaving in the morning, too," Jessie said. "And

we sure as the devil don't need these people to get to Tucson."

"Don't be so sure of that," the sheriff said darkly.

Frank Ranger looked up at Ki. "You sucker-punched me," he said, pushing himself unsteadily to his feet.

"Uh-uh," Ki replied, "It was a 'knife-hand blow,' not a 'sucker punch.' And if you'd like to see another martial arts blow, then come on and take a swing at me."

Frank Ranger cursed and did swing his meaty fist. Ki ducked, danced back, and then his right foot shot out and drove deeply into Ranger's midsection. Everyone in the stage office saw the man's cheeks balloon outward as he doubled up and then dropped back to his knees, struggling for air.

Ki's dark eyes took in each of the other stageline employees. When he was satisfied that none of them wanted a similar demonstration, he relaxed and then followed Jessie out the door.

"I'll get you for this!" Frank Ranger screeched. "We'll see how well you use a six-gun the next time we meet!"

Ki heard the threat but did not allow it to concern him. Any man who was so ignorant as to confuse a Japanese-American with a Chinaman was not to be taken very seriously, even if he did own a stageline.

★

Chapter 3

Early the next morning, when Jessie and Ki were preparing to leave, a boy of about thirteen rode up before the livery. Jessie noticed him immediately because he was riding a burro and wore a faded serape, wide sombrero, and rope sandals. The boy's feet were dirty, his hair was long and unwashed, and his pants were far too short and quite frayed.

"Excuse me, señorita," he said very formally as he removed the old, sweat-stained sombrero out of which some horse or perhaps his own burro had taken a generous bite. To her surprise, Jessie saw that the boy's hair was dark brown and not black. He was not a Mexican, but perhaps a half-breed. "But I hear you are going to Tucson."

Jessie, who had just finished saddling her horse and was tying a refilled canteen to her saddle horn, said, "Who told you that?"

"The man who owns the stageline. He told me that if I wanted to go to Tucson, I could go with you because I did not have enough money to buy a ticket."

"Oh, no," Jessie said, "you can't go with us."

The boy slipped off his burro. He was considerably taller than Jessie had first supposed, and she judged him to be about thirteen.

"Señorita," he said, bowing slightly. "It is a matter of great importance to me to go to Tucson at once."

"I'm sure that it is," Jessie said, noting the boy's earnestness. "It's just that the Apache are raiding north of the border just now. I'm sure you have heard of the renegade named Tatano."

"I have, señorita," he said, reaching under his serape for an ancient percussion Colt, which he proudly displayed as if it would surely convince her that he was a man to be reckoned with in all matters. "As you can see, Ricardo Miguel Escobar Smith is prepared for any and all troubles."

If the boy had not been so serious about himself and the situation, Jessie would have laughed outright. But something told her this ragged boy was trying very hard to be a man and doing a fine job of it despite circumstances. It was clear that he was poor and ill-fed, probably illiterate, and yet he had been raised with a sense of responsibility and honor.

Jessie glanced at the samurai, who merely shrugged his shoulders in a question. She turned back to the boy. "You say your name is Ricardo Smith?"

"*Sí*, señorita," he told her as he pulled back his serape and tried to hide the fact that his holster was just a piece of stiff rawhide and his belt nothing but a rope.

"And why, Ricardo, is it so important for you to get to Tucson in such a hurry?"

"It is my mother, señorita. She is dying, and I must meet my father before she is gone, so that he can help my family."

18

"You must *meet* him?"

"*Sí.*" The boy nodded vigorously. "I am told he is a very rich and important man. Very important. He will help my family. But only if I tell him how poor my mother is and how many children he has."

Jessie did not understand. "How could he not know you and his other children?"

The boy's eyes dropped to the ground, and Jessie saw his lips move soundlessly. "I . . . I am not able to tell you this, señorita. It is a matter of great personal sadness. My family lives in Juárez. Señor Smith, he would send for her sometimes and he loved her very much. He. . . ."

"I understand," Jessie said quickly. "The past is not important. It is the present that concerns me. Has your mother seen a doctor?"

"Oh *sí*! She has seen a doctor and he sent for the priest. My mother is dying. I know this. The doctor and the priest know this, too."

Jessie's heart ached to hear this story. Here was a boy trying to be a man, willing to risk his life to reach a father that he did not know, had never even been allowed to see. What his mother had no doubt been was a rich man's mistress. And now, sick and dying, the boy had some sad illusion that his father, who had denied the existence of his children, would help his illegitimate family. Smith! No doubt the man had even fabricated his name so that he could not be held legally responsible for his Mexican mistress and his bastard offspring.

"Are you the oldest, Ricardo?" Jessie asked, forgetting for the moment her desire to be on the trail for Tucson.

"*Sí.* I am the man of the family."

"That is obvious," Jessie said with genuine admiration. "And what will you tell your father if you find him?"

19

"I will tell him that my mother has never had another man in love. Not ever. And I will tell him that, besides myself, there is little Rosa."

"I see."

"Look," Ricardo said, reaching into his serape and producing a neatly folded note. "It is from my mother to my father begging him to come to her and to help us. I have read this letter. It speaks from the heart. I know my father will hear and he will come to Juárez."

"Maybe *I* can help your mother," Jessie said.

"Only God can help her, señorita."

"But maybe God and another doctor," Jessie said stubbornly. "I will find another doctor to see her this morning."

Ricardo's eyes grew wide with wonder. "You would do this for us!"

"*Sí.* I mean, yes. We would do this for you and your family."

Ricardo turned his head away quickly, and Jessie heard an unbidden sob escape his throat. She put an arm around his shoulder. "You are a son to make any woman proud, Ricardo Smith."

He leaned against her side for just a moment before he straightened up, walked back to his burro, and jumped on its thin back. "We go when you are ready, señorita."

"Tucson can wait another couple of hours," Jessie said to Ki. "It won't take any longer than that."

"Don't be too sure of it," Ki said.

Jessie finished tying her canteen down, and then she mounted Sun. "Let's go, hombre," she said to the boy.

Ricardo's chin lifted, and he drove the heels of his sandals into the ribs of his poor burro. The animal laid back its ears and tried to swing its head around and bite Ricardo's legs, but the boy prevented this by hauling back on his reins. He pulled a long stick out of his serape and applied it liberally to the burro's rump, sending the animal braying out the barn door.

"This one is quite a young man, isn't he?" Jessie said, mounting her horse.

"He is for a fact," Ki said.

Jessie looked into the samurai's eyes. "I'll make a confession, Ki. The boy reminds me of what you might have been like after being orphaned in Japan, then ostracized by the native Japanese people because of your American father's blood."

"I was also thin before the great *ronin*, Hirata, took me in and taught me *kakuto bugei*, the true samurai's ways. But I never had a burro. If I had, I would have killed and eaten it."

Jessie managed a smile. "Let's go see the woman and see if she could use the services of another doctor. There is no telling what kind of medical advice a family that poor would receive. I have seen Juárez on the other side of the Rio Grande. It is pitiable."

Ki followed Jessie and the boy out the barn door, and they rode side by side through the still-quiet streets of El Paso. He could not help but keep glancing at Ricardo Smith and be similarly reminded of his own impoverished and desperate childhood.

Ki's mother had been a beautiful Japanese woman of noble ancestry, but after marrying an American sea captain, who then suddenly took ill and died, she became an outcast. The Japanese, like the Chinese and most Orientals, considered all other races inferior, and Ki, the product of a mixed union, might have actually starved to death if he had not been saved by the great samurai, Hirata, himself an outcast after his master had died.

Jessie had not been thinking about anything but the boy and his family, but suddenly a stagecoach came swinging around the corner.

"Hi-yah!" the driver yelled, whipping the six horses forward. It was Frank Ranger, and when he saw Ki and Jessie, he did not grab for the brake or make any attempt to avoid a collision.

Jessie and Ki, mounted on quick horses, were able to get out of the stagecoach's way, but poor Ricardo Smith, on the little burro, did not fare as well. The burro did make an attempt to escape, but it was struck a powerful, glancing blow by the wagon's rear wheel.

"Ricardo!" Jessie cried, throwing herself from her saddle as the burro and the boy were slammed down in the street.

Ricardo was dazed. His thin leg was trapped under the burro, which was thrashing and trying to come to its feet despite the fact that its two front legs were horribly mutilated and one was twisted at a crazy angle.

"Migelo!" the boy murmured, trying to touch and calm the thrashing mule.

Jessie and Ki each grabbed the burro's legs and pulled it away from the boy before the pain-crazed animal did serious damage to Ricardo.

"Are you all right?" Jessie asked, kneeling beside the boy.

"*Sí*, señorita, but my Migelo. He is hurt very bad, eh?"

Jessie glanced over her shoulder. "Yes. His right front leg is broken. He must be killed or he will suffer."

"No!"

Jessie took a deep breath. "Ricardo!" she said sharply. "The burro will never walk. It is in great pain. You, being a man, will know that it must be killed now."

Ricardo's eyes filled with tears. He twisted around so that he could see the suffering burro, and he closed his eyes tightly, tears flowing down his cheeks.

"*Sí*," he whispered. "Hurry, please, señorita."

Jessie drew her six-gun. "I wish this bullet was for Frank Ranger instead," she stated.

Jessie's gun exploded, and the burro died instantly. Someone had called for a doctor, and one was already striding down the street.

"I need to see that leg," the doctor said, reaching into his medical bag and bringing out a pair of scissors.

Ricardo pulled his leg away. "Is okay, Doctor."

"Yeah, probably so, but I still want to see it."

"No, not if you cut my pants!"

The doctor looked at Jessie. "Lady, this kid might have a broken leg and be so excited that he doesn't even realize it. Just to make sure, I should look at it!"

"Ricardo," Jessie said, "I will buy you a new pair of pants. These are a boy's pants and you are a man now. You have outgrown them."

Ricardo relaxed, and the doctor quickly cut the pants up to a place above the knee. He carefully examined the leg, his fingers gentle and yet very competent.

"Can you bend your knee, young man?"

Ricardo nodded and bent his knee, but everyone could tell by his expression that it wasn't easy.

"Well?" Jessie asked.

"He's lucky. No broken bones, torn knee ligaments, or ruptured blood vessels. His leg is just very badly bruised. It'll be a few days before he should put much weight on it."

"Doctor, what is your name?"

"Collins. Dr. Homer Collins."

Without wasting any words, Jessie explained to the doctor about Ricardo's mother. "I will pay you twenty-five dollars to come with us right now and make a house call."

"Twenty-five dollars?"

"If it isn't enough, then. . . ."

"Oh, hell no!" the doctor protested. "That's more money than I make in a week sometimes. I'd just finished hitching up my buggy. We can take the boy in that."

"Will it ford the Rio Grande?" Ki asked.

"Only one way to find out," the doctor replied.

Fifteen minutes later, the doctor was whipping his buggy horse across the shallow river and into Mexico with Ricardo Smith pointing the way south toward some distant hovels crowded near the riverbank.

"I like this man," Jessie said, "and I sure hope that he can help Ricardo's mother."

"So do I," the samurai offered.

Maria Escobar Smith, as she proudly called herself, was lying on a thin corn-husk pallet near her door, and when she saw the carriage roll up before her decrepit hovel, she pushed herself to her hands and knees and tried to stand, but she was so weak that when she did get to her feet, she had to cling to the door in order not to fall.

"For God's sake!" the doctor cried, jumping from his buggy and running to grab the woman before she pitched over on her face. "Mrs. Smith, you should be in a hospital, not lying on the floor of this place."

"It is my home," she said, "and that being the case, who are you?"

"I'm Dr. Collins. Your boy had a bad fall, but he's going to be fine."

At just that moment, Ricardo managed to hobble to the poor shack and kneel by his mother's side. "I have brought

24

help much faster than you expected, eh, Mother? The Lord must be finally listening to our prayers."

"He has always listened," the woman said with a wan smile. "And I hear him calling me now."

Ricardo shook his head back and forth. "This is not so. Or . . . or if you hear His voice, He is telling you to stay here with us."

"What is wrong?" the doctor asked, looking down into the woman's face, which was still quite beautiful despite being ravaged by a long, unremitting pain.

"I have a pain inside," she told him.

"Where?"

Maria Smith touched a place just over her abdomen. "Here."

"May I examine it?"

Maria blinked. "You mean touch me?"

"Yes. It's very important."

Maria thought about it for a moment, and Jessie could almost read her mind. She could tell that the poor woman was resigned to dying and thought that an examination was just needless embarrassment.

"If not for yourself," Jessie said, "then for your children."

"*Sí*," Maria said quietly. "For the children."

Jessie, Ki, and Ricardo went outside to stand on the bank of the river. All around them there were half-naked Mexican children playing. There were also countless flea-infested dogs, several goats, and a number of burros.

"I will miss Migelo very, very much," Ricardo said wistfully. "He hated my guts, but we had a very good understanding, he and I. I was the boss when I had a stick; when I had no stick, he was the boss." Ricardo looked up at them. "Why did that man drive his stagecoach into us?"

25

"Because he is mean and vicious," Jessie said.

"I will make him pay for the burro many times over," Ki promised, "when I find him in Tucson. The only thing that will keep me from him is if he is first killed by the Apache."

Ricardo and Jessie could see that the samurai was not making an idle threat.

Nearly an hour passed while they waited, watching the children, the dogs, and the the old women who sat squatting before their own little hovels, staring at them and the activity on the American side of the river.

At last, Dr. Collins emerged, and he looked serious but not defeated. "I think she has a gall or kidney stone causing her a great deal of pain."

"Can you treat her?"

"If that's what it is, yes. It's a matter of diet. She has to take medicine and drink plenty of water to dissolve the stone. She cannot continue to drink goat's milk—or any milk for that matter."

"So what is there to do?" Jessie asked.

"We have to take her across the river and to a hotel. A good, clean hotel where she can be kept under close observation."

"I want to pay for it," Jessie said.

The doctor smiled for the first time. He was rather a handsome man, though a little weary looking. "I was hoping you might offer. Certainly there is no way that Mrs. Smith could help defray the cost. So if you pay for the room and board for her and her children, I'll offer my services and medicine free."

"You are very generous."

"I married a Mexican woman and took her from circumstances not much better than this. She died in childbirth

26

seven years ago. We would have had a girl like Rosa."

"I'm sorry."

"So am I," the doctor said. "After my wife's death, I went back to the East to medical school and now, seeing Mrs. Smith, I am once more reminded of why I became a doctor. It sure as the devil hasn't been for the money."

Jessie smiled and made a mental note to have Circle Star send this man a generous check for his kindness. A check that would pay many times over his expenses.

Maria was not at all sure about leaving her little shack by the river. It took Jessie, Ricardo, and the doctor to finally convince her that she might not die and that she needed to be taken good care of in a clean place with good, wholesome food. In the end, it was seven-year-old Rosa, who hugged her mother's neck and begged to go with them, that turned the tide and convinced Maria that she owed her children this chance.

By the time they had the Smith family in a hotel room close to the doctor's office and Jessie had made all the arrangements to have the hotel bill her at the Circle Star Ranch for as long as Maria needed care, it was evening and the day was finished. They repaired to the dining room.

"We will leave at dawn," Jessie said.

"We shall see," Ki told her.

"I am coming with you if I have to walk to Tucson," Ricardo vowed.

"No!"

"*Sí!*"

It was a standoff. Jessie tried to think of some way to convince this headstrong man-boy that there was nothing to be gained by risking his life in making some hopeless

27

journey to find a father that would not acknowledge his wife, his daughter, or a fine son.

"Maybe I can find him for you," Jessie said.

But Ricardo shook his head. "It is for *me* to do."

"Well then will you at least wait until this Tatano and his warriors have been captured?"

"I cannot."

"But you heard the doctor!" Jessie said with exasperation. "He said that your mother might not die yet! She's still very young and—"

"The other doctor said she would die. And so did the priest. I cannot take the chance. *Comprendes*?"

"Dammit!" Jessie snorted with exasperation. "You are very headstrong and you are not thinking clearly."

Ricardo looked away. "Thank you for the meal," he said finally. "I have never had so much food. And now, I must go take some to my mother and to Rosa. If I don't see you in the morning, *adiós*."

Jessie and Ki watched helplessly as Ricardo swept almost all of his steak and fried potatoes, along with a slice of apple pie, into his cloth napkin, which he carefully folded and then stuffed into his faded serape before hobbling painfully away.

"He hardly ate anything."

"I know," Jessie said. "He saved nearly everything for his mother and sister. I think he'd even have saved his glass of milk if he could have figured a way."

"So what are you going to do about tomorrow?"

"We leave very early."

Ki nodded but without any enthusiasm. "I do not think that will change his mind. He will find a way to come after us. Nothing will stop him except death. He might even steal a horse."

28

"Do you think so?"

"Yes. I know that boy because I was once like him. You said that, remember?"

"Of course." Jessie toyed with her own slice of apple pie. "So what are you suggesting?"

"Nothing," the samurai said. "I am merely telling you that he will follow us until he drops."

Jessie sighed and stared into her coffee cup. "In that case, we'd better take him. I'll have to buy another horse. A fast and strong one that can outrun an Apache pony."

"That would be a good idea," Ki said, suppressing a grin because he very much approved and also wanted to help the tough, determined little Ricardo Smith.

★

Chapter 4

It took nearly two hours the next morning to find exactly the right horse for Ricardo and then a saddle and the supplies he'd need to accompany them on the long, hard journey to Tucson.

When they finally had the horse ready, Jessie said, "I'll go up to his hotel room and tell him we've changed our minds. I want to say good-bye to his mother and Rosa anyway."

"The boy will need some new britches and other clothing," Ki reminded her.

"The general store will be our last stop before we leave town. It's better because that way, Ricardo can decide what fits and what does not. I want to buy him a pair of new cowboys boots, too."

"Don't overdo it," Ki advised. "It's not good to take a boy who's lived his entire life with nothing and then suddenly shower him with gifts."

"He can't get those Mexican sandals through a pair of stirrups with any degree of safety," Jessie said. "They'd slip

30

through, and he could be thrown and dragged to death."

"I know," the samurai said, "but again, too much too soon is not good for the boy."

Having stated his opinion, Ki put his mind to other matters. He never argued with Jessie, but he thought that perhaps she, having never been poor, did not quite understand the situation.

"I'll be right back," Jessie said when they rode up to the hotel.

A few minutes later she was banging on the door and hearing Rosa's sweet little voice asking who was there. Jessie smiled. "It's me, Señorita Starbuck. May I come in?"

Jessie heard Maria's voice, and then the door opened to reveal the little girl with her big dark eyes shining proudly for Jessie's inspection. Rosa stood up on her toes and preened with happiness, and Jessie could tell the little girl was going to be a beauty, as her mother had once been. This morning, Rosa was clean, her hair was brushed, and she was wearing a new pink dress with white lace. She reminded Jessie of a little angel.

Jessie bent down to look into the pretty girl's eyes. "You are beautiful!"

Rosa fairly shook with joy. "And my mother is feeling much better!"

Jessie went over to the bed. "How are you this morning, Mrs. Smith?"

"I feel good."

"You look much better." Jessie pulled a chair up beside the bed. "Where is Ricardo?"

"He is gone," Maria said, her eyes misting. "He left for Tucson last night after bringing us some food."

Jessie was shocked and dismayed. "He's already gone?"

31

"*Sí*. He is very determined, that one. He gets it from his father."

Jessie had been about to jump up and leave to find the boy, but now she hesitated. "Mrs. Smith, is there any chance that he will actually locate his father?"

"Oh, *sí*! Señor Smith is a very important man in Tucson. He has much money. It was he who paid for our English lessons. He said that someday, we would all come live in his big house in Arizona."

"But he never sent for you?"

"Oh, *sí*! I went there . . . five, maybe six times. Once each year at first, then . . . not so often."

"But never with the children."

Maria looked quickly away but not before Jessie saw the pain in her eyes. "They were never invited. Señor Smith, he said he was no good around little children. He said that someday . . ."

Maria's words trailed off and her eyes grew distant. It seemed obvious to Jessie that, even to Maria, the lie had become so hollow and painful that it was impossible to speak of it any longer.

"I see," Jessie said quickly, "but he knows of them?"

Maria nodded. "He even helped to name them."

"But he never sent for them," Jessie said, unable to hide the disapproval in her voice. "And he never helped you to raise them."

"He paid for the English lessons," Maria said stubbornly. "Ricardo can read and write, too. And Rosa, she is very smart. Smarter than I am, for sure."

Jessie stood up. The very last thing in the world she wanted to do was to pry into this woman's life, but she had a few more questions that needed to be asked.

"Mrs. Smith, what is your husband's first name?"

"Señor Richard. Ricardo is named after his father."

"And where does he live?"

"In Tucson."

"Yes, but exactly where in Tucson?"

Maria's lips formed a thin, uncompromising line. "I . . . I don't know this," she said finally. "I always stayed at a very nice hotel. He came to see me at night and also during the day. At first, before Rosa was born, he sometimes brought me flowers and other presents. Later, he just . . . just came for short visits."

"I see." Jessie saw all too well. "Do you remember the hotel where you stayed?"

"Hotel Blanca."

"The white hotel?"

"*Si!*" Maria smiled. "Have you seen it, Señorita Starbuck?"

Jessie nodded. Hotel Blanca was a sleazy, rundown hotel in the poorest part of Tucson. Of course, to this poor woman, it would have seemed like a palace. But it was the kind of a place where a man would bring a woman when he did not want to be seen by his peers.

"It is very beautiful, no?"

"Yes," Jessie forced herself to say. "Is there anything else you can tell me to help find this man?"

"He is a . . . how you say it?"

"I don't know."

"He makes the laws."

"He's a judge?"

"No."

"A lawyer, then?"

Maria shrugged her thin shoulders. "He is very important and he is rich. I think he is . . . what you call it?"

"A lawyer. An attorney."

"*Sí!* An attorney! This is what he called himself."

"I don't suppose you have a picture of Mr. Richard Smith."

Maria shook her head. "But I draw pictures of him to show my children. I bring one with me here. You want to see?"

"Very much."

Maria brought a picture out of her purse. It was drawn on smudged and torn paper and looked quite old, but the drawing was excellent.

"You draw this?"

"*Sí.*"

"You are very talented, Maria. Do you have others?"

"*Sí.*"

"May I keep this one to help me find your husband, the father of your children?"

Maria hesitated for a moment, then nodded her head.

"I must go now," Jessie said, slipping a hundred dollars into Maria's purse as she placed it back by her beside. "And you must do everything the doctor says. You promise?"

"I promise. But I think I will still die."

"I don't think so," Jessie said, "and neither does Dr. Collins."

Jessie hugged Rosa and left quickly. She hurried downstairs and out to the horses.

"He left last night. Probably soon after he delivered his dinner to his mother and sister."

"On foot with that bad leg?"

Jessie shook her head. "As you and I agreed, Ricardo Smith is a very, very determined young man."

Ki nodded grimly. "Then we must catch him with his new horse before he becomes a very dead man."

• • •

As he hobbled along the dusty road comforted only by his old percussion pistol, the most valuable thing owned by his family, Ricardo Smith wished very much for Migelo, his poor dead burro. To keep his mind from the constant pain in his leg, he recalled stories of the burro. How he had found it in a barranca many miles from the village and how it had been caught in a bog during the rainy season.

"He would have died then," Ricardo told himself once again, "and he knew that he owed his life to me alone."

Migelo *had* known. And while the ill-tempered little beast had often kicked and bit Ricardo, the kicks were never very hard and the bites were more like nips. But with anyone else . . . well, Migelo would kick and bite very, very hard. Ricardo had only to remember the time that someone had tried to sneak into his little pole corral behind their adobe hut and steal Migelo in the darkness of the night.

Oh, what a scream the man had made! Migelo, probably half-asleep and then startled and thus very angry, had kicked and bitten the man so many times he had been unable to escape. Many of Ricardo's neighbors had come, and they had caught the man and tied him to a tree. In the morning, the neighbors had wanted to whip the thief, but Ricardo's mother had forbidden this, saying that the poor man had already been harshly punished by Migelo.

Ricardo smiled to remember how everyone had agreed. And so, where only the day before everyone had thought that Migelo was a terrible burro, now, the little fellow had become a celebrity! Other children had looked upon Ricardo and the most famous burro in Juárez with admiration instead of scorn.

On the currents of wind high above, a buzzard sailed across the hard, arid land and cast an eye down at the hobbling boy, some primordial sense within its brain telling it that this might be a meal as it weakened under the sun. The buzzard sailed and soared, its black shadow streaking across the landscape faster than an Apache arrow and just as sinisterly.

Ricardo stopped and removed his sombrero. He sleeved his forehead with a fold of his serape, uncorked a gourd, and drank the water of the Rio Grande before he pulled the sombrero down close over his eyes and continued down the deserted wagon tracks. When the memory of Migelo brought an ache to his throat, he turned his thoughts to his mother and his sister.

This new line of thinking made him much happier. Perhaps his mother was not going to die after all. Perhaps even priests could make mistakes, because, while they were very close to God, they were men after all. Ricardo thought this was true, and he remembered the kind Dr. Collins and how the man had examined his leg and seemed so sure and confident of himself. He was, Ricardo thought, much better than the Mexican doctor with the powerful smell of tequila on his breath.

By mid-afternoon, Ricardo could go no farther. The sun was very hot and his leg was throbbing fiercely, so he sat down in the shade of a clump of brush and stretched his legs out before him. The vast silence that surrounded him would have unnerved many grown men, but not Ricardo. Since early childhood, he had taken comfort in exploring the desert solitudes both north and south of the Rio Grande.

"You are wasting your time," he told the buzzard, which had dropped several hundred feet and was watching him with growing interest. "Tatano might get me, but you won't."

Almost as if it heard and understood, the buzzard wheeled upward on a thermal draft and sailed south across the border,

36

back into Mexico, but Ricardo saw that it never went quite out of his vision, because the specter of death was always real and present in this cruel, unforgiving land.

An hour later Jessie and Ki overtook the boy and roused him from a deep slumber.

"Ricardo?"

He awakened with a start. "Señorita Starbuck! Señor Ki!"

"Are you all right?" Ki asked, his hands involuntarily moving over the boy's knee.

Ricardo flinched but smiled. "*Sí!* I am good now. Very good!"

"We have a horse for you."

Ricardo's brown eyes grew wide. "For me!"

"Yes," Jessie said. "And a saddle and supplies so that you can go with us to Tucson."

Ricardo rubbed his eyes and stared at them, then the horse, as if he could not quite believe his ears.

He pushed himself to his feet and hobbled over to the fine little sorrel mare that Jessie had bought for him. "*This* horse?" he asked, shaking his head with disbelief.

"Yes," Jessie said. "Do you like her?"

"She is almost as beautiful as you, señorita!"

Even Ki laughed at that. "And wait until you open those packages tied behind your saddle."

"*My* saddle!"

"Uh-huh," Jessie said. "Your saddle."

Ricardo ran his hands over the saddle. "Is it new?"

"No," Jessie said. "But almost."

"It is new to me," Ricardo said, his eyes full of the horse and the saddle, his hands moving over both in a loving caress.

The boy was so taken with his new horse and saddle, he didn't even want to open the packages, so Ki opened them for him. It took twenty minutes for Ricardo to dress in his new pants, shirt, and boots.

"When we come to another general store, if you want, I will buy you a Stetson to replace that sombrero," Jessie said.

"I cannot think of words to say enough thank you," Ricardo whispered. "I will forever be in your debt. I do not know . . ."

"*Nada*," Jessie interrupted, "it is nothing. Maybe someday you will come to work for me in Texas. Learn to be a proud vaquero. The mare is young. You have much to learn, but so does she."

Ricardo threw his rope belt and rawhide holster away and stuck his pistol behind the waistband of his new, stiff jeans. "They were a little loose, señorita," he said. "But with the gun, they are perfect."

"Are you any good with it?" Ki asked.

In reply, Ricardo pulled the Colt out, aimed at a rock in the road, and fired. The percussion pistol belched smoke and fire, and Jessie saw the ball miss the rock by at least five feet.

Waving the smoke aside and squinting at the rock, Ricardo said, "I hit it, no?"

"No," Jessie said. "May I see your pistol?"

Ricardo handed it to her. "Be very careful, señorita. It's a fine weapon, but a little touchy. Sometimes it shoots, sometimes not. But I am sure, in a fight, it will not fail."

Jessie was not so sure at all. The front sight was knocked half off; the handle, which had once been walnut, had been cracked and, to hold it together, had been wrapped with wire; and two cylinders had been stuffed with small, cylindrical pieces of wood so that they could not be fired for reasons that Jessie did not even want to imagine.

Still, Ricardo seemed so proud of the weapon that when she handed it back to him, she did not have the heart to say it was nearly useless.

"It is a fine gun," she said, "but perhaps we might also find you another."

"What for?"

"Well, just to back this one up," Jessie said. "Many men carry two pistols in Apache country."

"But Ki does not carry even one," the boy argued. "I think you should buy him one first."

"I do not need a gun," Ki said. "I have different weapons. Samurai weapons."

"You need a gun to protect this beautiful woman, Señor Ki," the boy said with a mild reproach. "But until then, you can use mine if I am killed."

Ki looked away and stifled a grin. When he turned back to the boy, he said, "You are very generous, Ricardo. If you are killed, then I will be happy to use yours."

Ricardo seemed pleased, and with his new boots and clothes, he was very proud as he climbed onto his new horse and saddle, then joined them on the road to Tucson, Arizona Territory.

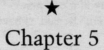

Chapter 5

Frank Ranger pulled impatiently on the brim of his Stetson and kicked the front wheel of his stagecoach with uncontrolled savagery.

"Shoot him!" he raged. "If the horse is lame, unhitch and shoot the stupid son of a bitch!"

The guard kneeling beside the right lead horse, a fine big bay, ran his hand up and down the sweaty animal's foreleg for about the twentieth time. "Be a damn shame."

"Austin, he's *my* damned horse!" Frank raged. "What the hell are you worried about! I'm the one that loses."

Austin stood up slowly. He was young but wide shouldered and strong. His hand never left the horse. "I care because this is a hell of a good animal and I don't think that there's one damn thing wrong with this animal's leg. I think he has a rock bruise."

"Rock bruise, bowed tendon," Frank said harshly, "what the hell is the difference out here in Apache country?"

"Well, the difference is that this animal might be able to

40

keep pulling the coach and we goddamn well might need him if there's trouble."

"Wrong!" Frank stood eye to eye with the younger man. "If there's trouble and we have to outrun the Apache, this bay horse will drag us down and hold us back. He'll be a liabilty that could endanger our lives. Now unhitch him like I said, lead him off a ways, and put him out of his misery! That's a damn order."

The horseman squinted his eyes. "Why don't you at least let me tie him to the back of the coach? If I do that, he can limp along behind, and if we're attacked, I can cut him free. And maybe he will make it to the next town, and then you can sell or trade him off to someone. Save you a lot of money. This is a valuable horse. A young, strong horse."

Frank shook his head. "Uh-uh," he said. "My horses either do what they're asked, or they're gone."

"Be reasonable, goddammit!" Austin swore. "This horse didn't ask to get a rock bruise. He's the best and the strongest animal out of the six."

"You gonna follow orders," Frank said, "or are you going to get fired and walk to Tucson!"

The younger man clenched his hands at his sides. He had never been spoken to in this manner, and he could hardly bear the thought of wasting such a fine animal as the bay. Sound, a youthful horse weighing over thirteen hundred pounds, was worth several hundred dollars in El Paso. The man had taken care of this horse along with all the others, and he liked them better than men—especially ones like his boss, Frank Ranger.

"I'll do it," Austin said, turning around to unhitch the fine bay gelding, "but it's a goddamn waste. A *stupid* goddamn waste!"

Frank Ranger laced his fingers together, raised his clenched fists, and sledgehammered a mighty blow to the base of Austin's neck. The tall young man shuddered and his legs buckled. He fell against the lame horse and grabbed its mane to keep from dropping to his knees. Frank unlaced his fingers and hit Austin again, and this time he dropped.

But Austin wasn't done for. Still conscious, he rolled under the lead horses and staggered erect on the other side of the team. His eyes were blurry and his head was spinning, but he could see Frank Ranger coming around the horses to finish him.

"You've always been a mouthy son of a bitch, and I should have whipped your ass months ago and then fired you," Frank hissed.

Austin raised his fists. "You come on and get it."

Frank Ranger came on strong. He waded in knowing that he did not want this fight to last very long, certainly not long enough for Austin to clear his head and steady his legs.

Frank landed a punch, took one in the face that rocked him back, then kicked Austin in the side of the knee, dropping him to the dirt.

They rolled, gouging, swearing, and punching, the other guards making a wide circle and watching in fixed silence. Everyone knew that Frank Ranger was tough and ruthless, that he was about the best fighter in El Paso, but Austin was giving the stageline owner his money's worth.

When they stopped rolling, Austin was astraddle his boss, big fists smashing into Ranger's face. Ranger's nose cracked and blood gushed over his face, but just when it appeared that he was finished, he kicked up with his boots and drove his spurs into Austin's cheeks, and then he yanked backward, tearing big chunks out of Austin's face. The younger man cried out in pain and grabbed his ripped and ruined face.

Ranger staggered to his feet, face covered with gore, eyes as wild and as merciless as those of a wolverine moving in for the kill.

"Boss, no!" a guard shouted.

But Ranger wasn't listening. He drew back his leg and kicked with all of his might, catching Austin in the throat and dropping him to writhe and choke in the dirt. Ranger jumped up and came down with both feet on Austin's chest, and then he got tangled up in his own spurs and fell across the stricken young horseman. When he recovered, he tore his gun from his holster and would have emptied his revolver into the younger man had the other guards not grabbed his Colt from his hands and pinned him against the coach.

"It's over!" a man shouted. "Frank, he's beaten!"

Ranger tried to tear lose because he wanted to stomp Austin again and drive the life from his body. But he was restrained long enough so that he came to his senses.

"Unhitch the damned horse!" He choked as he spoke.

Men jumped to obey his orders. Ranger smeared the blood across his face with the back of his sleeve and climbed into the coach and slammed the door.

"Let's roll!" he shouted.

"But what about Austin! We can't just leave him choking here in the dirt!"

Ranger tore his gun free and shoved it through the leather curtain. "You either do as you're ordered, or you can join him in hell!"

The man who had spoken had no trouble at all making his next decision, and within minutes, they were rolling on down the wagon track, dust rooster-tailing up to the sky.

For a long time, Austin thought he was going to die. He could not get his breath because his throat was so badly damaged that it swelled up and almost choked off every last bit of his air. And had he panicked and become hysterical, he would have died. But Austin wasn't ready to die, and so he forced himself to lie very still in a pool of agony and concentrate on taking one desperate lungful of air at a time.

He could not move, and the sun burned his face and nearly blinded him, but after a while, the sun went down and the earth cooled. It was just at sundown when he felt something touch his hand and he pulled it away quickly, certain that it was a rattlesnake or perhaps a scorpion or tarantula.

But it was none of those things. The huge bay gelding nuzzled him again, its nostrils twitching at the smell of blood but its mind telling it that this was a man who had often curried and fed it and had always been kind.

Austin tried to speak, but his voice was a tortured whisper. "So it's you," he said. "I should have let him put you down for keeps. Better you than me, horse."

The bay nickered softly and nuzzled the man again. It was hungry and lonesome.

"Go away."

But the animal did not go away. It stood beside the man all night long, and all morning, when Austin stood because it was either stand or die. The horse seemed grateful. It had been cut from its harness, and Austin used it to pull himself onto the horse's back. He had a raging thirst and his chest felt broken.

"Let's go," he wheezed. When the horse tried to turn and head for its stall in El Paso, Austin wrenched its head around.

"No!" he croaked. "We're going to find Frank Ranger, and I'll kill him if it's the very last thing I ever do."

The horse tossed its head, unhappy at going west and at the pain in its hoof. But Austin was insistent, and the bay plodded along the road, its mind more and more concerned with water.

Late that afternoon, Austin lost consciousness and tumbled from the bay. He was finished. There was no way that he could climb back on the horse, and he was in no condition to stand, let alone walk. Staring up into the sky, he saw a buzzard wheeling against an endless blue backdrop.

"Stick around," he whispered, "because I think you're going to have a meal of me by tomorrow."

The buzzard moved a little closer, and Austin listened as the bay gelding turned and limped off toward El Paso.

Ki saw the horse first. "Look!"

"What's a lone horse doing out here?" Jessie asked.

Ki shrugged and they galloped ahead to find out. When they saw that the animal was lame and wearing the harness of a lead wagon horse, there were still more unanswered questions.

"Why'd they cut it loose like that instead of tying it to the wagon and trying to get it to a horse doctor in the next town?" Jessie asked, more to herself than to the others.

Ki examined the horse. "Rock bruise."

Jessie frowned. "I wonder how far ahead of us they are."

Ki studied the wheel marks. "Maybe a day. Maybe not quite that far. We'll catch them."

Jessie and Ricardo exchanged glances because the tone of Ki's voice left no doubt that when they did overtake Frank

45

Ranger, there would be a showdown.

"If we leave the horse out here, it will never live to reach water," Jessie said, studying the fine animal. "It's much too fine a horse to allow to suffer."

"So what do you want to do?" Ki asked.

"We'll take it with us and hope that we can reach water before it drops. If it falls, we can put it out of its misery then."

Ki approved and caught the horse, tying it to his own mount. He knew that Jessie would push on until they did find water, even if that meant riding all night.

Ki was not mistaken. It was nearly two in the morning when they saw a man lying in the road and trotted up to investigate.

"He's still alive but in bad shape," Ki said, taking the big man's pulse.

Jessie put the opening of her canteen to Austin's lips and poured a little water. In a moment, the prostrate man was trying to tear the canteen out of her hands and satisfy what must have been a raging thirst.

"Easy," Jessie said. "Easy."

But the man was strong and half-crazed with thirst, and he managed to choke down almost half of the water left in her canteen before she could get it away from him.

"What happened to you?"

He looked up at her, and when he spoke, his voice grated like tin against a rock. "It was Ranger. I turned my back on him, and he hit me so hard I never got back into the fight. It was over a lame horse."

"Yeah," Jessie said, "we met him walking toward us in the moonlight. Is there any water close up ahead?"

"About six miles is all." The man gripped Jessie's arm so hard it pained her. "Are you going to leave me to die?"

46

"If I was, I sure wouldn't have given you what was in my canteen, now would I?"

Austin managed a smile. His face was battered and one eye was swollen closed. His chest was on fire and his throat hurt to speak, but he choked, "You help me to live, I'll kill him for you, ma'am."

"I think Ki has first claim on that pleasure," Jessie said. "But you can take that up with him later. Right now, we need to get you on your feet and onto that lame horse. He won't get us six miles in any big hurry, but we'll be there long before daylight."

Austin nodded, and they managed to get him back on the horse. "Here," Jessie said, handing him her canteen. "There's still a few swallows."

"What about you?"

"I can wait."

But Austin shook his head. "If you can wait, then so can I."

"There's no sense in arriving there with water in our canteens," Jessie said impatiently. "So go ahead and drink."

Austin drank the canteen dry. "Thank you, ma'am. I ought to be ashamed of myself for doing that, but I ain't."

Jessie climbed on Sun. "Just hang on until we stop for rest and water," she said. "And as for Frank Ranger, well, he's got to stop once in a while himself, and maybe, just maybe, he'll run a little interference for us with the Apache."

"Lordy!" Austin whispered, "now that would be justice. Maybe old Geronimo himself will skewer Frank. And if not him, then Tatano."

"Better them than us, señor," Ricardo said solemnly.

Austin nodded. He wondered why this beautiful angel of mercy that had just saved his life was traveling with a Chinaman and a Mexican boy. It made a man wonder what

47

would happen if *they* were the ones that were jumped by Apache.

If that happens, Austin thought dejectedly as he studied Ki's strange bow and Ricardo's old percussion pistol, which looked as if it would explode in the boy's fist, I guess we're as good as goners.

★

Chapter 6

Frank Ranger pulled out of Indian Wells with a well-watered team of horses and three barrels of water strapped to the back of his stagecoach. The track he followed took a sharp turn to the north.

"If we can make it through the next hundred miles to the Gila River, we'll follow it right into Tucson and we'll be all right," he said. "But between us and the Gila is some hard, dangerous country."

"It can't be any harder or worse than what we've come through so far," a guard said, staring back at what had once been a stage station but had long since been burned out by the Apache. "I'm just damn glad that the Indians didn't poison that well."

"They need the water as bad as we do," Frank growled, peering out through the windows of his coach.

The guard studied Frank closely. "How come we don't just take the Army payroll and turn this thing around?"

Frank looked across the hot, dusty interior of the coach.

"I gave that some thought," he admitted, "but if we did that, we'd all be hunted down by the Pinkertons, the Army, and every other law organization you can think of. Unless a man ran off to South America or something, it wouldn't be worth the risk."

"In South America, they have women with soft brown bodies. We'd be rich Americanos."

"Probably dead Americanos, soon enough," Frank said. "No, I've got too much to lose."

"I don't," the guard said. "I got nothing to lose but my life."

Frank felt himself grow tense inside. He had been afraid of this conversation. If this man had been making this talk among the other guards, it could lead to some very bad decisions.

"How much is in that strongbox?" the guard asked, trying to keep his voice sounding light.

"Not much."

"Aww! Come on now! You didn't hire six guards and decide to risk your own life for peanuts. I'll bet there's a hundred thousand dollars in that strongbox. Maybe even more."

A coldness filled Frank Ranger's chest, and he felt his heart quicken. "You really think so?"

"I do!" the guard said with a wink.

"Well, you're wrong."

The guard's smile faded and his voice took on an edge. "If I'm wrong, why don't you prove it and open the strong-box so we can all see how much money we're risking our lives for? You got the key."

"Yeah," Frank said, "I do. But that box stays sealed and you know what?"

"What?"

Frank raised his left hand and crooked his finger, motioning the man to lean forward as if he were going to whisper a secret. The guard leaned forward, but he didn't hear a secret. Instead, he grunted and collapsed forward between the seats as the barrel of Frank's gun split his skull wide open.

Frank opened the door and shoved the body out of the racing stagecoach. It struck the ground, actually bounced, and then rolled over and over to a stop. Frank looked up, but no one on top had heard a thing, and he knew the driver and the four remaining guards were unaware that another of their number had been disposed of.

Frank quietly closed the door. He threw his feet up on the cushion opposite himself and removed from his coat pocket a long, twisted cheroot, which he lit and inhaled deeply.

Two guards and one horse shy of what he had left El Paso with, Frank scowled out at the barren countryside of southeastern Arizona. It was a damn shame to lose two decent fighting men, but both had become dangerous to his own well-being. In his experience, Frank had found that a man could not afford to show any weakness to either his enemies or his employees. Weakness encouraged boldness, and boldness was dangerous among other men.

Frank smoked his cheroot with a thoughtful look in his eyes. He would be glad when he finally reached Tucson, and he would not return to El Paso until he could do it accompanied by a large company of United States Cavalry. It would be folly to attempt this crossing twice with only a stage, five weary horses, and a few good marksmen.

Frank supposed that he had been dozing. No one could blame a man for that. The coach had been pulling up a long hill, and it was hot, at least ninety degrees, when the

51

first Apache scream split the suffocating desert air and was closely followed by a volley of rifle shots.

A man atop the coach barked a cry of pain, and then Frank saw the guard drop past his window. He heard the driver's whip cracking furiously, but the hill was much too long and steep to pull at any speed.

Frank stuck his head out the door and saw that the Apache were attacking from both sides of the road. There looked to be at least thirty of them. He looked ahead and saw that they were still a good hundred yards from the crest of the hill.

Frank swore as he grabbed his Winchester, shoved it through the window, and took aim on a mounted Indian. He fired, but the coach was bouncing so violently that he missed and had to fire a second time in order to drop the Indian. He could hear his guards firing rapidly up on the roof, and he knew that they would be stretched out and making every shot count.

The coach seemed to creep up the hill with agonizing slowness as the Indians swept past on their laboring ponies. Frank's Winchester barked death, but after he had knocked two more Apache from their horses, the Indians turned their rifles toward his window, and had he not thrown himself on the floor and stayed there, he would have been riddled.

"Mr. Ranger!" a guard cried. "Mr. Ranger, the driver's been hit!"

Frank yanked his six-gun from his holster and kicked open the door. He waited a moment, until the warriors swept by and the way out was momentarily clear, and then he scrambled out of the coach, falling headfirst to the ground and very nearly getting himself run over by the rear wheels.

A couple of wild bullets kicked dirt in his face, and then he was up and racing to the horses, grabbing the lines and using them to whip the laboring animals into a shambling run.

"Cover me!" he shouted, glancing up at the coach and seeing only two guards still firing.

Somehow, the coach crested the hill, and then gravity was suddenly in its favor. The horses threw themselves even more earnestly into their harness, and the coach gathered speed. Frank jammed his six-gun into his holster and tried desperately to pull himself up to the box while somehow hanging onto the precious driving lines.

He was clawing at the side of the coach when it hit a sharp mountainside curve and rocked up on two wheels. Frank was jerked high into the air. He thought the coach would make it around the curve, but he was wrong, and with a sickening slowness, the Concord coach dropped over onto its side and crashed, then skidded to a shuddering halt.

Frank was thrown into the air, and when he landed, he felt something in his back snap. He tried to yell for help from his guards, but his voice was only a whisper. He could hear the Apache, but above even their terrible screams, he heard the pitiful screams of his broken stage horses as they thrashed in the tangle of chains and harness.

"Help," he whispered, fingers reaching for his gun.

An Apache suddenly loomed over him. Frank screeched and managed to yank his gun out of its holster, but the Apache stepped on his wrist and then lowered the barrel of his rifle to Frank's face.

The Indian was grinning! The dirty son of a bitch was actually enjoying this moment!

Frank cursed and tried to spit up at the man, but his mouth was as dry as the dust where he lay squirming, and when he opened his mouth to curse, the Apache shoved the barrel of his smoking rifle into Frank's mouth.

Horror flooded through his half-paralyzed body, and Frank's eyes bugged and he began to choke as the barrel was rammed down his throat, the front sights tearing tissue and filling his mouth with blood. The Apache laughed, and Frank's hand slapped the breech of the rifle as he tried to reach and pull the trigger.

The Apache, realizing his wishes, saved him the trouble, and when the rifle shook, Frank saw a crimson explosion behind his eyes and then nothing.

Jessie drank deeply from the water at Indian Wells, and so did the others. "We'll spend the night and move on in the morning," she announced. "The horses need a rest and so do we."

No one complained or objected. It was pretty obvious that they'd find Frank Ranger and his stagecoach in Tucson or burned to ashes somewhere up ahead. It made no sense at all to push their horses until they were too weak to be spirited away from a superior force of Apache.

Late that evening, they made a small campfire and Ki, accompanied by Ricardo, went out hunting. Jessie knew the samurai would find them meat to kill with his bow and arrows.

"What kind of a man is he, anyway?" Austin said, breaking into Jessie's thoughts. "I heard he whipped up on Frank Ranger. Take it from me, that's no easy thing to do."

Jessie looked at the big man across the fire. "Ki is a samurai, a Japanese warrior."

"He sure packs a funny-looking bow," Austin said. "And

I heard he uses his hands and his feet in a fight."

"He does," Jessie said. "He is also trained as a *Ninja*."

"As what?"

"*Ninja*." Jessie quickly explained how a *Ninja* was trained to be an invisible assassin. How they were taught to use every available shadow, every piece of cover, to sneak up and kill their enemies. She finished by saying, "Ki is more dangerous than any Apache."

"Hard to believe."

"Believe it," Jessie said. "I would not be alive today if not for Ki."

Austin was silent for several moments. Then he said, "Are you and him . . . well. . . ."

"No," Jessie said. "He serves me as a companion, protector, and friend. It is the way of the samurai to serve, rather than to be served."

"Hmm," Austin said. "Maybe he would teach me a few of them kicks and chops that he used on Ranger. I could have used them the other day."

"From what you told us," Jessie said, "your mistake was in turning your back on the man."

"Yeah, that, and standing up for a lame horse."

"I find that very admirable," Jessie said, favoring the young man with a smile. "No one else apparently thought enough of a good horse to try and save its life."

"I like horses better than people," Austin admitted. "People are mostly mean, and I don't understand them very well. But horses . . . well, I talk their language. I've been around them since I was toddling around in diapers. I even like the outlaw horses."

"I could use you on Circle Star in Texas," Jessie said. "If you ever want a job breaking and training good horses, come see me in Texas."

"What part, ma'am?"

"West Texas. Just say Circle Star and people will give you directions."

Austin looked at her for several moments. "It's that big, huh?"

"Yes, it is."

A short time later, Ki and Ricardo returned with several cottontail rabbits. Ricardo could not stop talking about how the samurai's bow spun completely around when fired and how Ki never missed.

Austin took this all in without a word, but late that evening when they were all ready to go to sleep, he leaned over and said, "Hey, samurai."

"What?"

"You think you could whip me?"

"Yes."

Jessie stiffened. She had sensed a little jealousy in Austin toward Ki. They were about the same age, but Austin was a good forty pounds and two inches bigger.

But Austin surprised her when he chuckled and said, "Hell, as beat up as I am, anyone could whip me, even Ricardo."

Jessie relaxed. Austin was rough, uncomplicated, and a good man. And more importantly, she thought that he was smart enough to realize that Ki really could whip him, even on his very best day.

The next afternoon, Jessie and her friends found the body of the first guard that Frank Ranger had shot and tossed from his coach.

"He did this," Austin swore. "Frank Ranger did this."

"Was this a good man?" Ki asked.

"Not very," Austin said.

"Then we will leave him."

Jessie did not object. The ground was rocky, and even if they'd had a pick and shovel, it would have taken a long time to dig a grave.

Hours later, they found another guard, and this one, it seemed likely, had been shot by the Apache, because he had been stripped of his boots and hat.

"I'm afraid of what we're going to find up ahead," Austin said quietly.

When they topped the hill and saw the ashes of the coach, the dead men and dead horses, Jessie looked away for a moment, then urged Sun on down the hill. No one had to say a word, because the skid marks showed where and how the coach had overturned.

"Well," Jessie said, staring down at Frank Ranger's corpse, "I guess this is one less problem we have to face up to when we reach Tucson."

Ki tore his eyes away form the carnage. "*If* we reach Tucson," he said quietly.

"How long ago did this happen?"

Ki dismounted and went over to the coach. He poked into the ashes, feeling their warmth. "Ten, twelve hours ago."

"I suppose the strongbox is missing," Jessie said.

"Yeah," Austin said, dismounting and going to the part of the coach where it would have been found. "It's gone."

Jessie stared at two dead wagon horses, and she supposed the other three had been taken away by the Apache. "Do you think it was Tantano?"

"Could be," Austin said. "And it might even have been Geronimo. There's no way we'll ever know for sure."

"Why don't we get out of here fast?" Jessie said, the stench of fire and death filling her nostrils.

No one argued with her. There was nothing to salvage here, so they mounted their horses and rode on, pushing the animals as hard as they dared and hoping that they could pass through this country alive.

★

Chapter 7

The Gila River was little more than a stream when they came upon it, but Jessie knew that in the early spring, the river could become a raging torrent. Birthed in the mountains of southwestern New Mexico, the Gila had long since been trapped out by the first mountain men, who had discovered the area more than fifty years earlier, and had become a trail for the settlers who traveled between the Rio Grande settlements and the Pacific Ocean. Once belonging to Mexico, the Gila River Basin had become United States Territory upon the signing of the Gadsden Purchase in 1853.

Periodically, gold had been discovered along the Gila River, but the strikes never lasted long and the Apache were so fierce and determined to hold their lands that anyone entering this country did so at extreme risk.

"At least we won't have to worry about water again," Ki said, giving his horse its reins so that it could drink deeply.

Jessie agreed. Next to avoiding Apache, finding water in this arid country was the most important factor in survival. Her eyes followed the river, studying the heavy stands of cottonwood trees whose roots sank far down into the mostly dry in search of water. The Gila River was also choked with salt cedar and stands of mesquite that could have hid a small army.

"The trouble is," she said, "we're not the only ones that will be sticking to the Gila. I'm sure that the Apache depend upon it for water as much as anyone."

"Are you saying that we should leave the river?" Austin asked.

"It might be a good idea," Jessie said. "During the daytime, we could ride parallel to it westward at a distance of three or four miles. At night, we could move in and water our horses and replenish our canteens, then ride out into the desert again."

"That makes good sense to me," Ki said.

Ricardo, who had been quiet most of that day, dared to voice his own opinion. "The Apache will spend the money they took from the stage on horses, women, guns, and whiskey. If there are towns along this river, perhaps that is where they will go."

"That's good thinking," Jessie said. "And there are a few places operating businesses along this river. Mostly, they're run by outlaws who trade with the renegade Apache and Mexican *bandidos* that move through this country raising hell."

"Then these are the places we ought to avoid," Austin said. "It's for darn sure that we can't recover the Army payroll that Frank was under contract to deliver to Tucson."

Jessie nodded. "Our main concern is to get to Tucson in one piece and try to help Pearl Appleton discover who killed her father and who is behind the death threats being made against Arizona judges."

"That's why we're going to Tucson?" Austin asked.

"That's why we're going," Jessie said. "We haven't heard your reasons yet."

Austin smiled. "I started out for Tucson because I was paid damn good money to help Ranger deliver the Army payroll. Then, after the fight, I vowed to find the man and settle the score."

"But now that he's dead, what is your reason?"

Austin scratched his chin. "Well, I guess the reason I'm tagging along with you folks is that I haven't got anything better to do and I'm not about to turn around and ride back to El Paso alone. I figure that if we stick together, we'll at least have a fighting chance if we're jumped by Apache."

"Frank Ranger and his guards never had one," Ki reminded the big man.

"Yeah," Austin said darkly, "but that big stagecoach left a trail of dust about mountain high. Any Apache within fifty miles would see it and come to investigate. But we're a different matter altogether. I figure that, with a little luck, we ought to be able to just slip on through."

No one said anything to that. They just finished letting their horses take all the water they could hold, and then they headed off to flank the river.

For two nights, their plan worked just fine, and then early one morning, before daybreak, when they sneaked down to the Gila to fill their canteens and water their horses in preparation for another long day in the saddle, Ki suddenly raised his hand in warning.

Without a word, he reined his pinto sharply into a heavy stand of salt cedar, and no one wasted any time asking foolish questions but went right after him.

They dismounted in the thickets and crowded in close to the samurai. "What is it?" Jessie asked.

"I heard a horse nicker somewhere just upriver," the samurai said. "Could be white men, but it's probably Apache."

Jessie pulled her Winchester from her saddle boot and tied her horse to a bush. "I guess we'd better get ready in case we're about to have a some trouble come riding up that riverbed." She turned to the samurai. "I suppose you'd like to scout ahead."

Ki nodded. He strung his bow and selected "Death's Song," the arrow with a ceramic bulb located just behind its head. The bulb had a hole drilled through it, and when "Death Song" was in flight, it made a terrible sound, one described by Jessie's dear friend, Longarm, as a match between the whine of the world's largest mosquito and a violin's strings being tortured.

"Maybe I should go with you," Austin said.

"Uh-uh," Ki told him. "Better you should stay here with Jessie and Ricardo."

"But hell, man, I can—"

"No," Ki said abruptly before he turned away.

"That samurai of yours is pretty damn bossy for a fella his size," Austin growled.

"He knows what he's doing," Jessie said, "and he knows that he can travel faster and quieter alone."

Ki heard that as he was moving off through the thickets, and then he closed his mind to everything except the task that lay before him.

The salt cedar and mesquite were too thick to ride a horse through, and even a man had to pick his way carefully along, but Ki did the best he could. Over long years of training, he'd developed a sort of sixth sense about trouble, and he knew that it was riding toward them now.

He heard another sound, stopped, and glanced down at his feet just in time to see a rattlesnake about as big around as his forearm poised to strike.

Ki froze and the rattles shivered. The diamondback was going to strike the moment he moved his foot, and now Ki could hear the sound of horse's hooves as they shuffled along the dry part of the riverbed.

He couldn't move his feet, so the samurai slipped his hand into his tunic and his fingers plucked a *shuriken* star blade. It was bigger and heavier than a silver dollar, but not much. Ki held it for a moment, and then, as the viper hissed and its forked tongue darted in and out, Ki gave his wrist a powerful flick to send the star blade flashing downward. It struck the reptile in the top of the head, and its lower points entered the viper's V-shaped skull to penetrate its evil little brain.

The rattler tried to strike even though mortally wounded. Its head, split as if by a cleaver, flashed toward Ki's foot, but the samurai jumped out of danger. The fangs of the dying serpent clamped down on the base of a bush, and Ki saw its yellowish venom squirt.

But the samurai was already moving into a crouch, and now he saw the Apache. There were eight of them. A small but very determined and very experienced band of fighters. Several of the Indians were leading heavily laden pack horses.

Ki immediately identified the leader, a warrior in his mid-thirties wearing a red bandana and riding a buckskin horse bigger and stronger than any of his companions. The leader held a Winchester rifle while his companions were armed with old single-shot carbines, probably taken from dead soldiers.

For one moment, Ki hesitated in some vain hope that the Apache might pass by and never notice the tracks of their enemies' horses. But that was impossible, so when the Indians passed, Ki slipped onto their backtrail and moved from cover to cover.

When the leader saw the tracks made by Jessie and her friends, he threw up his arm and shouted something, and that's when Jessie, Austin, and Ricardo opened fire.

Three Indians were knocked from their saddles, but the leader managed to whirl his horse around and try to escape in order to regroup.

Ki was waiting. He saw the lead warrior raise his rifle and fire, but the samurai coolly fitted "Death Song" on his bowstring, then drew it back to his ear. An Apache bullet whip-cracked past his cheek, and Ki unleashed "Death Song." The arrow screeched like a dying thing, and Ki saw the Apache leader's eyes open wide with fear and amazement before the ceramic bulb exploded against his chest and then vanished into his heart.

The next few moments were chaos with rifles firing so quickly that they sounded as if they were a rolling thunder. Ki caught a glimpse of Ricardo with his big old pistol clenched in his little fists as he emptied his weapon, raising a huge cloud of white gunsmoke but missing every one of the Apache.

The samurai sent another arrow flashing, and it brought a second Apache down, and when a third wheeled his horse and came at the samurai, Ki jumped to the side and another *shuriken* star blade flashed through the air and embedded itself in the warrior's forehead.

A moment later, two wounded Apache were racing off into the brush and the battle was over. For perhaps a full second, no one moved or said a word. A packhorse snorted and stomped its feet nervously in the Gila River.

Jessie was the first one to speak. "Is anyone hurt?"

"No, ma'am," Austin said.

"No, señorita."

"Good." Jessie expelled a deep sigh. "Let's catch up to those packhorses and get out of here just in case there are any more Apache within the sound of gunfire."

"You'll get no arguments on that from me," Austin said, jumping into action.

Ricardo gathered himself. He looked disgusted with his old percussion gun, which had only brought down one Apache in the first volley.

"Señorita?"

"Yes?"

"Do you mind if I take an Indian gun and rifle?"

"I think that would be a fine idea," Jessie told the boy. "I take it that you are ready for a change."

"*Sí.*" Ricardo held the old pistol up before his eyes. "This gun is . . . how you say it?"

"Worthless."

"*Sí!* Worthless."

Ricardo hurled the empty old Colt into the brush and went to strip the weapons from the dead Indians in the hope of finding a better pistol and a good rifle.

"Next time, señorita," he promised, "I will do much better."

"You did just fine. You brought down a warrior in that first volley."

"*Sí,*" Ricardo said with disgust, "but not the one I aimed at."

★

Chapter 8

Tucson was a very old town. It had been founded by the Spaniards as the Presidio San Agustin de Tucson in 1775, named after a nearby Papago village. During its first century, Tucson had been sacked many times by the fierce Apache, but by the time that Jessie, Ki, Ricardo, and Austin arrived, Tucson had grown large enough to defend itself against any invaders. With a population numbering more than ten thousand, Tucson could boast with great pride at the growth of its community and the fact that it had become the territorial capitol of Arizona.

As Jessie approached the bustling distribution center, she noted the irrigated fields, and just on the edge of town there was a huge sign that read, TUCSON WELCOMES THE SOUTHERN PACIFIC RAILROAD IN 1880!

"I have always liked Tucson," Austin said. "Could be that I might just settle down here and plant some roots."

"You could hardly find a better place," Jessie said. "The town is booming, partly because of news that the Southern

Pacific will be coming but also because of the gold and silver discoveries in Bisbee and Tombstone. If you ask me, Tucson would be a good place to invest in some land."

"You've never said why you've risked your lives to get here," Austin said, looking first at Jessie, then at Ki.

"It's a personal matter," Jessie said. "As I told you, it involves an old friend of my father whose name was Judge Stanley Appleton. He was murdered, and there have been several other judges murdered in the Arizona Territory as well. The letter I received in Texas was written by the Appleton's daughter. Pearl has also been threatened, and that's why we were in such a hurry to get here."

Austin frowned. "And nobody has any idea who is behind this?"

"Apparently not," Jessie said.

"Mind if I sort of tag along?" Austin asked. "Maybe I can keep my own nose to the ground and scare up some useful information, seeing as I how I plan to stick around Tucson for a while."

"Any and all help will be appreciated," Jessie said.

Ricardo Smith was almost bouncing in his saddle with excitement as they entered the town. Jessie, Ki, and even Austin, who knew the boy's sad story, exchanged worried glances. None of them wished to see Ricardo's heart broken.

It was for this reason that Jessie reined her horse up for a moment and said, "Ricardo, just a minute please. We need to talk."

The boy didn't want to talk. Anyone could see that. His eyes kept darting here and there, bouncing off one stranger's face to leap to that of another, hoping that he would see his father.

"Ricardo," Jessie said, her voice firm, "I want you to

promise me that you will not expect too much from your father. I mean, after all, you have never seen him before and there is no telling what you might find."

"He is tall, rich, and handsome," Ricardo said in a rush. "I have a picture of him, and I know that when he learns my mother is in need, he will return with me to El Paso."

"But if he doesn't," Jessie said, her voice softening. "If he is not quite as good a man as you hope, then . . ."

Ricardo shook his head violently. "Señorita Starbuck," he said, "you have been more than good to me. All of you have. You give me a horse, clothes, food, everything. But please, do not speak of my father in a bad way."

Before Jessie could form a reply, Ricardo had spotted Hotel Blanca one block south of Main Street. The hotel had once been glistening white, but now it was dull and gray with dust. If Ricardo noticed, he said nothing but turned his horse in that direction.

"I must go to find my father now," he said, "but I will visit you later. You must meet my father. I will tell him how brave and how good you were to me."

"I look forward to meeting him very much," Jessie said, smiling but having a difficult time hiding the disapproval she felt toward a man who would make so many promises to a family that he had never even had the courage or character to publically acknowledge.

"Would you mind if Ki helped you to find your father?" Jessie asked.

Ricardo did not look too pleased at the offer, but he so admired the samurai that he could not object. "Thank you, Señor Ki. Your help would be appreciated."

"It's settled then," Jessie said. "Ki, I'll be staying at the Hotel Brockton just down the street, and I'll have a room reserved for you next to mine, if possible. For right now, however, Austin and I will go see Pearl."

The samurai nodded and Jessie turned to Austin. "Let's go find Pearl and just hope that we have not arrived too late."

Austin looked grim. "What kind of men would kill a judge and then threaten to murder his daughter?"

"I don't know," Jessie said. "But I mean to find out."

When they arrived at Judge Appleton's stately old frame mansion on Grande Avenue, Jessie and Austin dismounted, tied their horses at the hitch rail, and batted a heavy layer of trail dust from their clothes.

"We look like we've ridden through hell," Austin said laconically. "And I guess, considering what we've been through to get here, we *have* ridden through hell."

"Pearl has never been the kind of person who judged people by their appearances," Jessie said. "She's a lot more sensible than that."

Austin scrubbed the two-day stubble on his cheeks. "I hope you're right."

Jessie noticed that the rose gardens that Judge Appleton had so loved suffered from neglect and the picket gate was in need of being rehung. And even though it was midday, the shades were drawn and the house somehow had a forlorn appearance.

Knocking on the door, she turned to Austin and said, "Miss Appleton and I did not spend much time together, but when I was passing through or she and the Judge were traveling in Texas, we always enjoyed eath other's company. As you will no doubt see, Pearl is the most generous person imaginable. To a fault, really, because she'll give away almost anything."

"That's pretty rare, all right," Austin said.

"I can tell you this because I know that you would never

take advantage of her generosity."

"Of course not!"

"Yes," Jessie said, "of course not. And I must quickly tell you something else about Pearl so that you will not be shocked."

"What's that?"

"Pearl was hurt very badly in a carriage accident that crushed her hip and left one of her legs partly paralyzed. She uses a cane when she tires."

"I wouldn't have said anything," Austin said, sounding hurt.

"I know that, but sometimes I think it is impossible for a stranger not to reflect a little shock at seeing someone so young and beautiful in such sad circumstances. Pearl, however, has never let her physical limitation affect her happiness. She is one of the most—"

The little iron gate window in the door opened, and a voice said, "Who is there?"

"It's Jessica Starbuck, of Texas. Is that you, Mildred?"

"Miss Starbuck, thank God!" Mildred cried as the door lock turned and an old woman opened her arms for Jessie.

"It is good to see you," Jessie said, hugging Mildred. "I'm sorry that we have taken so long to reach Tucson. It's a long, not very pleasant story that can wait." Jessie pulled back. "This is Austin," she said. "He's a friend of mine and a very valuable one."

"We can use all the friends we can get," Mildred said, her smile evaporating.

"Is Pearl upstairs?"

"Yes." Mildred's eyes misted. "I'm afraid she's not doing too well, Miss Jessica. Just yesterday, she got another one of those notes that said that she either had to pay ten thousand dollars, or she'd be killed."

Jessie's eyes grew flinty. "So, now they are trying extortion."

Mildred nodded. She leaned close to Jessie. "Miss Pearl is about done in over worry. First there was the grieving for her father, now this. She don't know what to do, and it's tearing that poor girl inside out."

"Mildred?" a fearful voice called from down the hallway. "Who was it? Is someone here? Answer me, Mildred."

Jessie started to move past the housekeeper but then froze as she saw Pearl lurch out of the parlor into the hallway.

"Mildred, please . . . Jessie!"

It almost broke Jessie's heart to see how badly Pearl had slipped. She had always been willowy and a little frail, but now she was so wraithlike that when Jessie held her, she could feel all of her bones.

"Thank heavens you have come!" Pearl whispered, burying her face in Jessie's hair and hugging her tightly. "I am at my wit's end."

Jessie held the young woman close. "It's going to be all right. We will end this siege of terror and find out who is behind the death of your father and bring that person—or persons—to justice."

Pearl looked past Jessie's shoulder at Austin, who was staring at them because he was not in the habit of seeing two strikingly beautiful women at the same time. And although it was dim in the hallway, he could see that both had tears in their eyes and that this was a very emotional reunion.

"You're not Ki," Pearl said.

"No, ma'am," he said, tearing his hat off and crunching it in his big fists. "My name is Peter Sedge Austin. Just Austin suits me fine."

Jessie disengaged herself. "Pearl, we met this man on the

trail out of El Paso. He fought at our side against Apache, and now he says he would like to help us find your father's murderer."

Pearl straightened. Only now did anyone notice how tall she actually was. Tall and quite stately but oh so very, very thin with dark circles under her tragic, filled eyes. Few daughters had adored their fathers as much as Pearl had loved Judge Austin. Her mother had died when she was very young, and Judge Appleton had never remarried, devoting himself to his daughter's welfare and the dispensation of justice in the new Arizona Territory.

"Mr. Austin," Pearl said, "any friend of Jessie's is a friend of mine. However, I must warn you that something here is very sinister and very dangerous. If you become involved in this matter, it could well cost you your life."

"I understand."

Pearl nodded. "Come into my father's library. Mildred, would you bring us some tea, unless, Mr. Austin, you would prefer something stronger."

"I might," Austin said agreeably.

"Brandy?"

Austin had probably been hoping for whiskey or even a decent tequila, but he would settle for brandy. "That would be fine, Miss Pearl."

The judge's library was something that would have made any scholarly man envious. It was wall-to-wall mahogany bookcases. And while the west end of the roughly twenty-foot-square library was filled with legal tomes, the remainder of the shelves were stuffed with the classics and a great many books on astronomy, history, and geology. There was also a special section on medicine read and reread by the judge during the agonizing years when he had sought in vain to find a way to restore full use of Pearl's right leg.

They sat in red velvet easy chairs, and Jessie noticed that Mildred lit kerosene lamps instead of opening the curtains, even though the judge's library windows looked out over a lovely backyard fenced for privacy.

Noticing Jessie's curiosity about using lamps in the middle of the daytime, Pearl explained. "It was just about this time of the day and in this very room that my father was murdered." Pearl pointed to the large easy chair where Austin had chosen to recline. "In fact, it was in that very chair you are sitting in now."

Austin started but was too proud to jump out of the chair and choose another. Pearl continued. "My father was reading in that chair when his assassin crept up to that open window and fired a single fatal shot. The bullet struck my father squarely between the eyes, and he pitched forward, facedown into a book."

Austin glanced at the shuttered window. "It would be an easy shot," he admitted.

"Yes," Pearl said. "My only consolation in this entire nightmare is that my father died instantly. He was in poor health at the time. In truth, he was suffering some internal malady that was wasting away his strength. The doctor was giving him laudanum."

"Laudanum?" Jessie asked, very aware that the opium-based drug was extremely powerful and used only as a last resort, usually in terminal cases where the individual was suffering intense and unremitting pain.

"Yes."

Mildred arrived so promptly with a tray of tea that Jessie suspected it had been brewed earlier.

"Your brandy, Mr. Austin," Mildred said, offering the man an unopened bottle of brandy bearing a fancy label and accompanied by a hand-cut crystal snifter.

Austin's eyes widened when he read the label. "Why this is *imported* brandy! It's from France."

Pearl raised her eyebrows with concern. "If you would prefer, I'm sure we can find some American brandy in my father's wine cellar. I don't know anything about such things. I'm sure that dear Mildred assumed, as I did, that one brandy was about as good as another."

"Oh, this will be splendid!" Austin said, opening the bottle and filling the snifter to the brim, then holding it up to the light and tossing the brandy down with relish.

He sighed, poured another glass, and this time smelled the bouquet. "I have never tasted or smelled anything so good outside of a . . . a rose garden," he amended.

Jessie could see quite plainly that his initial analogy had been discarded, probably because it had to do with loose women. Austin looked quite uncomfortable right then, and he tossed down the second glass of brandy.

"My," Pearl said, "I'm so glad that you approve. My father was considered a connoisseur of fine liquor and tobacco."

"He most certainly was," Austin said, "but I can't say I care much for this little bitty glass."

"Fine brandy is to be sipped," Jessie said, "not swilled down like beer."

"Oh." Austin shifted uncomfortably.

"Would you care to try one of my father's favorite Cuban cigars, Mr. Austin?" Pearl asked.

"You dam . . . rned right I would."

"Mildred?"

Mildred was far more worldly than Pearl, and she could tell that Austin was not a gentleman of refinement. Still, Pearl was the boss in her father's house, so Mildred brought in an airtight walnut case of imported cigars and opened the

74

lid, exposing them for Austin's inspection.

"Wow!" he exclaimed. "These sure aren't your everyday garden variety of Mexican twisters, that's for certain! Mind if I try a couple?"

"Of course not," Pearl said. "Mildred and I certainly won't be smoking them."

Austin avoided both Jessie's and Mildred's disapproving look and snatched up a thick handful of the cigars. He found a match in his pocket, stuffed the extra cigars in another shirt pocket, lit the first one, inhaled deeply, and then sighed with pleasure.

"You approve?" Pearl asked.

"Best cigar I've ever smoked," the young man said. "After this, my Saturday night cheroots are going to taste mighty humble."

"Well, then you should take a few more and come back when those are gone," Mildred said.

Austin might have taken her up on the offer, but Jessie's eyes made him keep his hands to himself, and after she had sipped her tea, she said, "Why don't you tell us all you know about your father's killer?"

"I don't know much of anything!" Pearl exclaimed. "The sheriff and his deputies have questioned everyone who knew my father. There are dozens of men whom he sentenced to the Arizona Territorial Prison in Yuma. Some of them were murderers. I don't know. Perhaps someone that has a grudge against my father has recently been paroled or has escaped."

"It would be worth checking into," Jessie said, making a mental note of it. "When did the notes asking for money start to arrive?"

"About two weeks ago."

"Perhaps we can set a trap."

"I suggested that to the sheriff, but he says it's too risky."

"It's also risky to just sit and do nothing," Jessie said. "Since we haven't a clue as to who is responsible, I think we have no choice but to try and lure them into a trap. And the only bait that will attract them appears to be money."

Pearl sighed. "I will do whatever you think best, Jessie. Did Ki come with you?"

"Yes." Very quickly, Jessie told her about Ricardo and his father.

"I know the man," Pearl said.

"You do?"

"Unfortunately. He's an attorney here in town. A rather well-to-do attorney who is looked upon with real disfavor by his peers. My father considered him an unethical man. And now, since my father's death, Richard Smith is campaigning with the territorial governor for my father's seat on the bench! Can you imagine the gall!"

"I can," Jessie said, "judging from what little I've already heard about the man, he has all the morals of an alley tomcat."

"He is corrupt and unscrupulous," Pearl said. "He is also a conceited fool who fancies himself a gift to all women. My father would cross the street rather than meet him."

Jessie shook her head. "I'm afraid that I'm going to have to meet the man very soon and have a serious heart-to-heart discussion with him concerning his filial obligations toward poor Ricardo and his mother."

"I should just love to see the snake's face when you do," Pearl said.

Jessie and Pearl talked a little more while Austin sat and listened, missing little as he enjoyed his rich Cuban cigar. After an hour, Jessie rose to leave.

"We have ridden a long, long way, and we are dirty and tired," she said. "We'll return tomorrow, and we can visit some more and lay plans for a trap."

Pearl nodded her head and swallowed nervously. It was obvious that the thought of enticing a killer with the promise of money scared her. But it was just as obvious that she was determined to bring this matter to a head and deliver to justice the ones responsible for her father's murder.

"You're a generous and a brave young lady," Austin said to Pearl as they stood on her porch. "Just meeting you has been a high honor and a supreme pleasure, Miss Appleton."

Pearl actually blushed at the handsome young man's compliment, and then he and Jessie mounted their horses and rode away.

★

Chapter 9

Ki did not have much faith that a shabby, run-down establishment like Hotel Blanca would prove helpful in finding Richard Smith. It was the kind of hotel that served either the poor, or so-called "respectable" married men who brought women here for a few hours of pleasure.

When Ki and Ricardo walked into the hotel they went right up to the front desk, and since there was no one present, Ki banged on the registration desk.

"I'm comin'. I'm comin'!" a voice crabbed from behind a door.

A moment later, a small, ferret-faced man in his sixties scuttled through the door and took his place behind the counter. "Rooms are a dollar a night, cash in advance."

"We do not want rooms, señor," Ricardo blurted, unable to curb his impatience. "I seek my father. His name is Señor Richard Smith."

"Mr. Smith don't live here! Hell, boy, a man like that wouldn't be caught dead in a place like this."

"But this is Hotel Blanca," Ricardo protested, "and my

mother, she described it to me many times."

Ricardo turned around and pointed to a chandelier that had long since seen its glory days and had obviously been shot to pieces by drunken cowboys.

"She told me about *that*, señor. And she said it was once very beautiful."

The hotel clerk stared up at the chandelier as if he'd never seen it before. "If it was ever beautiful," he said, "it was before I came to work here, and that was five years ago."

Ricardo turned back to the man. "Do you know this Señor Richard Smith?"

"Everyone knows him. He's campaigning to be the judge in this county. What has that got to do with anything?"

"He is my father, señor."

The desk clerk blinked. "Now what the hell ever gave a little Mexican brat like you that idea?"

Ki reached across the desk and grabbed the small, ill-tempered man. "I think you had better be careful not to insult my young friend," he warned. "Ricardo has come a long way and seen much danger in order to meet his father."

"Let go of me!" the man shrieked. "If you lay an hand on me, I'll call the sheriff and he'll throw your yellow ass in jail!"

Ki seriously debated whether or not to teach this foul man a lesson in manners but decided that it would not be worth the effort. Old men like this were too set in their ways. They either aged well, or they went sour.

"Let's go," Ki said.

"But what about my father!"

"If he is running for an office as important as judge, we will have no trouble finding him very quickly."

Ricardo nodded, and Ki could see the lad was crestfallen

as he looked around the hotel once again. "Ever since I was a little boy, my mother told me about this place. She said it was very beautiful. She told me about that chandelier and about how this place was always white as fresh snow, inside and out. She said the carpets were so soft that it felt like walking on pillows."

Ricardo looked down at the filthy, threadbare carpet. "My mother would not lie," he whispered, "but it has been a long time since she was here. Like our family, Hotel Blanca has fallen on very bad times."

"Yes," Ki said, taking Ricardo's arm. "I'm afraid it has."

The hotel clerk waited until they reached the front door. He had overheard Ricardo's sad comments, and they must have touched what small part was left of his heart.

"Hey, kid!"

Ricardo turned around. "*Sí?*"

"Mr. Smith has an office two blocks north of here. It's right beside the bank of Tucson. Handsome brick building. You can't miss it."

Ricardo's chin lifted. "Thank you, señor!"

"You'll thank me now," the desk clerk said before he turned away, "but you won't be so quick to thank me after you meet him."

Before Ricardo could say anything more, Ki took him outside and they headed for the man's office.

"Ricardo?"

"*Sí?*"

"You heard what the man at the hotel said about your father. Perhaps it would be better if you let me or Jessie speak to him first. That way, we could—"

"No!" Ricardo lowered his voice. "I am sorry, Señor Ki. But he *is* my father. The only one I have. I must meet him

80

man to man and speak of my mother. Even if he is not all that I had hoped, surely he will help my mother and poor sister. If he is a good man, he will send for them."

Ki said nothing more as they walked along. He was very sure in his heart that Richard Smith was anything but a "good man," and yet, he could understand why the boy felt he must be the one to confront his father after so many years of waiting.

As promised, the attorney's office was impressive, and a heavy brass plate on the door bore the ornate inscription RICHARD SMITH, ATTORNEY AT LAW. Ki watched the boy read the plaque and when Ricardo swallowed noisily and hesitated, he wondered at the boy's thoughts. Was Ricardo at last coming face-to-face with his illusion and now afraid to learn the truth about his father?

"What is wrong?" Ki asked.

"Maybe . . . maybe we should come back later, señor."

"Why?"

Ricardo struggled. "I just think that this might not be a good time. I could take a bath and we . . ."

Ki squatted down on his heels. "Listen to me," he said quietly. "Because your skin is brown and mine is, too, and because we are both a mixture of two races—half-breeds, as the ignorant refer to us—all our lives there are some people who are going to try and tell us that we are not as good as they are. You must not listen to those people. You must never start thinking that anyone is any better or worse than we are simply because they have blue eyes or have more money."

Ricardo glanced again at the plaque. "But, señor . . ."

"Drop the 'señor' and 'señorita'," Ki ordered. "You are in the United States now. When I first came to this country, I had to drop my Japanese phrases, but I kept what was important to me of my own culture and traditions. As you can see, I am a samurai and I dress differently and think differently, but when I speak, I speak English. You must do the same in order to gain respect."

"I am afraid of him," Ricardo said miserably.

"Only," Ki said, "because you are afraid of what he will say or do that might hurt your feelings. But if you know that your value depends on what you are *inside* instead of on the outside, then you can look any man in the eye."

"But what can I tell my mother if he . . . he does not love her?"

"You must tell her the truth. And your little sister, too, when she is old enough to understand." Ki stood up. "Your father can't hurt us; he can only hurt himself by behaving badly. We will go to him in an honorable way, and then he must in turn treat us with respect."

Ricardo took a deep breath and expelled it slowly. He removed his battered sombrero and held it at his side. "I am ready."

Ki had never had a son, but if he had, he would have wished for him to be like Ricardo Smith. Having never known his own father, the samurai believed he could understand a little of how Ricardo would feel to at last meet his American father. It would take some courage, the kind that Ricardo was showing right now.

"Good," Ki said as he pushed open the door and lead the way inside.

The room was spacious and extremely ornate. The carpets were imported from Persia, and the chandeliers were the kind that Maria Smith had lovingly described for her poor children as they grew up in the dirt and poverty of Juárez. There was a hand-carved wooden railing and gate that separated the entry from the office itself, and when Ki and Ricardo entered, a clerk with a green eyeshade looked up. Seeing the two dusty brown vistors, he scowled with disapproval and came to his feet.

"What possible business can you have in this establishment?"

Ki was looking past the clerk to a wood- and glass-enclosed office where two men were engaged in a private conversation.

"That is him," Ricardo whispered, pulling out the drawing that his mother had made and holding it up for comparison. "That is him!"

The clerk glanced over his shoulder. "That is whom?"

"Mr. Richard Smith," Ki said when Ricardo could not answer but stared with an open mouth at the silver-haired and very dignified-looking gentleman in a perfectly tailored suit.

"Of course it is!" the clerk snapped. "But what is the purpose of your visit, or are you simply lost or—"

"We need to see him right now," Ki said, cutting the man off in mid-sentence.

"Impossible. That man that he is speaking with is our territorial governor, Mr. Hatfield."

"Come on," Ki said, starting to push through the gate.

"Stop!" the clerk hissed. "Just who do you think you are, barging in here without an appointment!"

"It's not who I am," Ki said tightly, "it's who this boy is. Now get out of my way."

The clerk looked stricken with indecision. He glanced over his shoulder and seemed to summon up enough resolve to stammer, "If . . . if you don't leave this very moment, I'll have you arrested and you will go to jail!"

In reply, the samurai reached out, and his thumb thrust powerfully into the flesh at the base of the clerk's collar.

The man's eyes dilated and then rolled up into his skull, and he collapsed on the fine carpet without a sound.

"How did you do that!" Ricardo exclaimed.

"Maybe I'll teach you someday," Ki said, shoving through the gate and heading for the lawyer's private office.

When Ki yanked open the attorney's door, Richard Smith and the territorial governor both looked startled, then upset.

The governor was a short, balding man with great bushy eyebrows and round, wire-rimmed glasses. He weighed no less than three hundred pounds. Smith, however, was tall and urbane, very handsome with a square jaw and an aquiline nose, both of which his son had inherited.

"What," Smith demanded, "is the meaning of this!"

Ricardo shrank back, but Ki stood his ground. "We have a very important reason for being here."

"It can't be important enough to interrupt this meeting," Smith said with asperity.

He stepped away from his desk to call his clerk, and that's when he saw the man lying on the carpet. Smith's eyes widened, and then he grabbed for his desk drawer, and Ki saw his hand clench around a gun. Before the man could take the gun from his drawer, the edge of Ki's palm slashed down and connected solidly with Smith's forearm. The gun exploded harmlessly into the drawer, and the governor was so startled that he flipped over backward in his chair, spilled across the carpet, and then went crabbing out the door, yelling for help.

Smith was not a man easily discouraged. Cursing, he made another try for the gun with his other hand, but Ki grabbed him by the lapels and slammed him down in his big leather office chair.

"Listen to me!" Ki shouted. "This is your son, Ricardo,

from Juárez, and he's got something to tell you about Maria."

Smith had been about to take a punch at Ki when the samurai's words froze him like a statue.

"What!"

"You heard me. This is your *son*."

Ki shoved the drawer closed so that Smith would not make another attempt at trying to reach his pistol. He watched as the lawyer's eyes bugged a little and he stared at Ricardo.

"You're Maria's boy?"

"*Sí*. I . . . I mean yes, sir. And you are my father."

Ricardo bowed slightly, and then he stuck out his hand and said in a trembling voice, "My father, I have waited these many years to have the honor of meeting you."

"What the hell are you doing here now!" Smith demanded.

Ricardo retreated a half step, and it almost broke the samurai's heart to see the pain in the boy's eyes as he stammered, "It is my mother. She is very sick and she needs help. We thought that if you would come to El Paso and—"

"You're crazy!" Smith jumped to his door. "Governor," he shouted, "it's all right. It's all right! I'll be right out."

Smith slammed the door shut so that they could not be heard. His handsome face was bloodless and his voice shook with fury. "Now you listen to me, both of you! I intend to be appointed to the bench in this territory! And for that to happen, I can't have any scandal about some unwashed bastard son from Mexico suddenly appearing to demand money."

"Enough," Ki said, his voice becoming icy. "You've said enough."

But the attorney had more to say. "How much you want,

85

Kid? How much to get the hell out of my life and out of this town and never come back?"

Ricardo began to tremble all over like a leaf in the wind. His eyes began to leak tears, and his lips were compressed in a thin, quavering line as he watched his father reach into his coat pocket, tear out a sheaf of greenbacks, and extend them.

"Here! There must be a hundred dollars. It'll pay for a doctor and medicine for your mother, or for her funeral. Just take the money and—"

Something snapped in the boy before it snapped in the samurai. With an animal sound, Ricardo hurled himself at his father, and he was tall enough to land a punch with his bony little fist that caught the attorney high on the chest. Money flew everywhere, and when the man cursed and grabbed a handful of Ricardo's hair, Ki struck a powerful *tegatana* blow that landed at the base of the man's neck and dropped him like rock in a river.

Smith's chin struck the edge of his desk, and the flesh was opened so that when he landed on the floor, he was bleeding heavily.

Ki did not care. "Let's go," he said. "I think we've seen all we need to see."

Ricardo nodded with agreement. He looked pale and shaken as they left the office and started for the front door.

"Hands up!"

Ki had been looking down at Ricardo and trying to think of something to say to the boy that would ease the pain he must have been feeling inside. But now, he looked up to see three lawmen filling the doorway, and their guns were drawn and aimed at his chest.

"Hands up or you're a dead man!" the one with the sheriff's badge shouted.

Ki stepped in front of Ricardo, because men sometimes did foolish things under pressure. Slowly, he raised his hands.

"Go see about Mr. Smith!" the sheriff ordered his deputies, who jumped forward and, careful to stay out of the line of fire, made their way into Smith's private office.

"He's badly hurt! Call a doctor!"

The sheriff relayed the call over his shoulder, and the gun shook in his hand. "Mister, I don't know what the hell you came here for, but I intend to find out, and my guess is that you'll be spending the next five or ten years in Yuma Prison. Maybe swing from a rope if Mr. Smith is dead."

"He's not dead," Ki said contemptuously. "He struck his chin on his desk when he fell."

"This way," the sheriff said, motioning with his gun. "Just come nice and easy. You too, boy. Say, is that a gun you're awearin' on your hip?"

"*Sí*, but—"

"Then reach across your belly and take it out, then drop it real slow. One false move, I'll put a hole in you the size of one of your mama's tortillas!"

Ki seethed with helpless fury as Ricardo did as ordered, and he protested, "The boy didn't hurt Smith. I did!"

"I'll decide who's going to jail, not you! Now raise your hands for the ceiling and come along peaceably, or I'll put a slug through you as big as a salt shaker!"

Ki ground his teeth in silence. He and Ricardo were marched out through an already large and growing crowd. A doctor rushed past him into the law office, and as Ki was marched past the territorial governor, he heard the fat man say, "It's for this kind of scum that we have built a new prison in Yuma. Let the sun and the heat down there boil the piss and vinegar out of him!"

"What about the boy?" someone asked.

"We'll see," the governor said, "but when he barged in with the Chinaman, he looked almost as dangerous. Better check him for a knife. Them greasers have always got 'em hidden somewhere under their clothes."

Ki was so frustrated he wanted to grab the governor and smash some justice and sense into his thick head. But with a gun poking him in the spine, Ki knew that he could do nothing.

"Ki?"

The samurai looked down at Ricardo. "Yeah?"

"Even if we hang," Ricardo said, "I am glad for what we did in there."

Ki lowered one hand and ruffled the boy's hair. "We won't hang. Jessie will get this straightened out. But I'm glad we acted as we did. And I'm glad you didn't take his damned money."

Ricardo's chin lifted. "I have never seen so much money in all my life. I . . . I confess, I was tempted."

"We're all tempted by things," Ki said, "and—"

"Shut up, get that arm up in the air, and walk faster!" the sheriff snarled as he jammed Ki painfully in the ribs. "You'll do your talking to a judge."

Ki clamped his mouth shut. He guessed he had not handled this very smoothly, but it had been a long, long time since he'd hit any man who deserved it more than Richard Smith.

★

Chapter 10

Jessie and Austin were riding their horses back from the Appleton house when they saw the large, excited crowd.

"Wonder what is going on," Austin said.

"Uh-oh," Jessie replied, spurring her horse forward into a trot. "They've got Ki and Ricardo under arrest."

When Jessie drew nearer, she decided that it would be wiser to wait until the sheriff and his deputies had put Ki and Ricardo in their jail rather than confront the peace officers in the street with so much commotion going on.

"What happened?" she asked the first man that she came to.

"There was some disturbance between those two men the sheriff has arrested and Mr. Smith, the lawyer who's seeking the appointment of judge. From what I hear, they beat the hell outa Smith. Somebody said he was bleedin' like a stuck hog."

Jessie dismounted and Austin did the same. They walked their horses along behind the crowd, and when they reached the sheriff's office, the sheriff pushed Ki and Ricardo inside.

"Y'all go on back to your business," the sheriff called. "There's nothin' worth gawkin' and fussin' over."

"What happened?" a big farmer demanded. "Mr. Smith was covered with blood. I'd say that was something important enough to know about."

"Mr. Smith was viciously attacked by the pair we have under arrest," the sheriff said. "Now I can't say any more than that. There will be a trial and it will all come out then. But until then, y'all best be getting back to your own business. The law has taken charge."

The sheriff turned and went back inside to join his deputies, slamming the door behind him.

"Damned half-breed Chinaman and a Mex boy is what did it," an old man grunted. "In my day, we'd have strung them sons-a-bitches up from the nearest tree!"

Jessie had to bite back a response. She started for the door, but Austin gently took hold of her arm. "Why don't we wait a few minutes until things simmer down? That sheriff, he looks about half-spooked to me. Let's let things calm down a half hour or so."

Jessie expelled a deep breath. "I suppose that's not bad thinking," she admitted. "And I am hungry."

"How about that little cafe over there?" Austin said, pointing to a place called TOM'S CAFE—GOOD FOOD AND DRINK.

"I was hoping for something a little nicer."

Austin grinned. "Hey," he said to a man standing close to them. "Is Tom's Cafe any good?"

"Cooks the best steaks and potatoes in Tucson. A little high on his prices, but . . ."

"No problem with that, huh, Jessie?"

He was grinning at her and she had to grin back. "I think we can come up with the money for a couple of steaks."

Austin threw an arm across Jessie's shoulders and steered her toward the cafe. He opened the door for her, and they sat down by the front window at a little table with a red-and-white checkered tablecloth.

"What'll it be?" a man said with a pleasant smile and sad blue eyes.

"You Tom?" Austin asked.

"I am."

"I think we'll have your specialty. Steak, potatoes and . . . ," Austin spied a pie under glass sitting on the counter, " . . . and that pie."

"All of it?"

"All of it," Austin said.

Tom looked at Jessie, his eyes showing some life for a moment. "Anything to drink, miss?"

"Milk for me."

"Beer for me," Austin said.

When Tom trudged off to cook their order, Jessie stared out the window toward the sheriff's office. Her brow was knitted with worry, and her mind was preoccupied with thoughts about Pearl as well as Ki and Ricardo.

"I have a very bad feeling about this town right now," she said. "And not just because there is a murderer and extortionist here bent on destroying the Appleton family, but also because of this business with Ricardo's father."

"It does appear to be getting smelly, don't it," Austin said. "I sure don't feel good about what poor Miss Appleton is going through. Why, living in that big house with all the windows curtained up so that she and old Mildred have to see by lamplight even in the daytime is the saddest thing I ever heard of. And they're both half scared to death."

"It sounds like they've got plenty of reason to be scared," Jessie said. "And the thing of it is, I'm not sure that there's anyone in this town that I'd trust to help us find out who is behind all this trouble."

"I don't see how we can avoid explaining things to the sheriff."

"Me neither," Jessie said, "but we sure haven't gotten off on the right foot with him, have we?"

"You mean with Ki and Ricardo being arrested?"

"Yeah."

"Let's look at the bright side," Austin said.

"Which is?"

Austin frowned. "I haven't come up with one yet," he said, "but I'm working on it."

The meal was slow in coming, but when Tom laid it before them, it was everything that the man on the street had promised. Jessie discovered that she was famished and even had room for a little apple pie. Tom had no difficulty eating the rest of it.

When the bill came, Tom put it in front of Austin, but Jessie paid. Tom said nothing, but Austin, as they were walking out, burped and said, "If you'd put me on the payroll, I'd treat your next meal."

"The payroll for what?"

"Oh, I don't know. Maybe protectin' you."

"I've got the samurai for that."

"Not when he's in jail you don't."

"Well," Jessie said, striking out across the street in her long-legged stride, "we're going to do something to change that right now."

Austin fell in beside her without a word. He'd seen Jessie in action against the Apache; now he was looking forward to seeing her in action against the sheriff of Tucson, Arizona.

"Whoever it is, tell 'em to come back tomorrow!" Jessie heard the sheriff roar from inside at one of his deputies, after she discovered the door was locked.

When the door opened, the deputy blinked at Jessie with a look of surprise that quickly turned to admiration. His scowl was replaced by a grin, and he tore his hat off and stammered, "Ma'am, I'm afraid the sheriff is busy just now, you'll have to come back tomorrow."

"I'm afraid that what I have to say won't wait that long," Jessie said, pushing past the surprised man.

"Now wait just a minute," the deputy said, grabbing Austin by the arm as he started to follow Jessie inside.

Austin pivoted and used his hip to throw the deputy out the door, completely over the boardwalk, and into the street. Then he followed Jessie inside.

"Now who the hell are you!" the sheriff raged.

Jessie wasted few words in explanation. "We came all the way from Texas to help Miss Pearl Appleton find out who murdered her father and who is threatening to murder her."

"Well, you can just drag your pretty behind right back to Texas!" the sheriff exclaimed. "This is Arizona Territory and this is *my* town. I run things here and I am the law."

"Well, you've done a mighty poor job of upholding the law if you can't find a murderer and an extortionist. Judge Appleton was one of your most prominent citizens, and I get the sense that you don't have a clue as to who murdered him in his own library."

"I think you'd better leave right now," the sheriff said, "before I arrest and throw you both in jail right alongside them other two."

93

"Ricardo is Richard Smith's son!"

"So he says," the sheriff sneered, "but he ain't the right color and he sure don't bear any resemblance to Mr. Smith. Not that I or any judge I know could see."

The sheriff turned around and marched to Ricardo's cell. He gripped the bars and glared at Ricardo. "You start telling everyone around that Mr. Smith is your father, you'll wind up in more trouble than you already are."

Ki moved toward the man, but Jessie's words hauled him up short. "No, Ki. That won't help matters."

"You're damn right it won't," the sheriff said, taking a back step just to be sure that the samurai could not reach through the bars and grab him.

Ki looked at Jessie. "So what happens now?"

"I'll tell you what happens," the sheriff interrupted. "Tomorrow, you'll be hauled in front of Judge J. Potter and sentenced to Yuma Prison for about five to ten years."

Jessie felt her heart sink. "I'll find a lawyer and we'll get this straightened out," she promised.

Ki nodded without much hope, because he could see the way the cards were falling from this stacked deck. "Ricardo didn't harm his father. He wanted to, and he got in one good punch, but it's wrong to hold him here in a jail cell."

"That's for Judge Potter to decide," the sheriff said. "The boy, I'll grant, is a little young for the territorial prison. We've got some real bad ones doing time in that hell hole. Maybe the judge will show the boy mercy, but he sure as hell is going to send you to prison, Chinaman. On that, you can bet your queue."

"I don't wear one," Ki said.

"Yeah, I can see that." The sheriff sneered. "Bet some big old cowboy cut the son of a bitch off. Don't that mean that if you die, you'll rot in a Chinaman's hell?"

Jessie had heard and seen enough. She marched up to the sheriff and slapped him across the face so hard his head rocked back and a trickle of blood ran from his lip.

"Ma'am," the sheriff choked, "before this is over, I'm going to see that you join the Chinaman in Yuma Prison. I swear that I will!"

Austin stepped forward, but Jessie grabbed his arm. "Let's just get out of here before we really get mad."

At the door, Jessie stopped and said, "We'll be at the courtroom tomorrow, Ki. I'll have the best lawyer money can buy, and we'll have all the ammunition we need to destroy Mr. Smith if he means to press for a prison sentence. I think, when he understands what the stakes are and what the charges could do to his chances of being made a judge, he might well decide to drop the charges."

"Ha!" the sheriff said. "Unless you've got proof about him being the boy's real father, you've got nothing but slander. The judge will throw the book at you and you'll go straight to prison."

"He couldn't do that."

"Don't bet on it," the sheriff said, his eyes turning mean and confident. "You see, Judge Potter is Mr. Smith's father-in-law."

One of the deputies, seeing the shocked looks on both Jessie and Austin's faces, burst out laughing.

But Jessie was looking at Ricardo, who had immediately begun to shake his head.

"But, señor, this cannot be true," he whispered. "You see, he is in love with my mother. He promised that, one day, he would marry her and bring our family to this town."

The deputy scoffed with derision. "Now what the hell would he have done with a Mexican woman and her brood of bastards! Why, your mother was nothing more to Mr. Smith than a—"

If Austin had not reached the deputy and knocked him to the floor before the man could say another word, Jessie would have. Austin hit the man so hard he slid ten feet across the worn wooden floor, and then the deputy's head cracked into the cell bars.

The sheriff drew his gun. "You're under arrest for assaulting a peace officer. Move and I'll gun you down!"

"Don't move!" Jessie cried, knowing that the sheriff and his remaining deputies really would kill Austin if he lost control of himself.

"Put up your hands!"

Austin did as he was told. His gun was removed from his holster, and a moment later he was shoved into the same cell with Ki and Ricardo. When the cell door locked, the sheriff wiped his hands together with satisfaction and turned to Jessie.

"Looks like all your friends are going to be heading for prison tomorrow."

"Think again," Jessie said, her voice shaking with rage.

She turned and headed for the door. It was all that Jessie could do to get out of the room before she drew her Colt and gunned down the whole rotten bunch.

★

Chapter 11

That evening, Jessie and Pearl went to visit an attorney named Rollin Adair in a seedy hotel on Sixth Street.

"I can't imagine hiring a man who would live in place like this," Jessie said as they waited in the lobby of the man's hotel and watched cockroaches scuttle around on the tobacco-stained bare wood floor.

"Rollin Adair is not what anyone would call a worldly success," Pearl admitted, "but the truth remains that he is the only lawyer who would dare oppose the sheriff and Richard Smith."

"Why? Because he's got nothing to lose?"

"Yes," Pearl said, "that's exactly the truth of it. And also because he once defended a Mexican who had been charged with raping and then murdering a white woman. And then he had the audacity to actually win his case and in such a convincing manner that Judge Potter had no choice but to set the Mexican free."

"And what was wrong with that?" Jessie asked.

"Everything," Pearl said. "The Mexican had a hard reputation. He was a known killer and even a gun runner for the

Apache. He should have been hung or sent to prison for a dozen reasons, and when he was acquitted on the charge he was arrested on, the town was furious. They caught the Mexican before he was able to get out of town, and they lynched him on the spot. Rollin Adair was there, and he blistered the crowd with his words. He said that they were wrong to lynch his client and that it made a mockery of the law."

"He had a point," Jessie said, "but so did the crowd."

"I know that," Pearl said. "You could argue it either way. The Mexican, whose name I forget, really deserved to die. He should have been arrested again and brought to trial on other charges. Adair told everyone that, but, with passions as high as they were that hot July afternoon, the crowd just lynched the Mexican."

"So this Rollin Adair not only flew in the face of public sentiment by winning freedom for the Mexican, he then chastised them for lynching the man and angered everyone."

"Exactly," Pearl said. "The mystery to me is why he has remained in Tucson. If he went away, he could practice law in any city he wanted. He's a graduate of Harvard and a very brilliant young man. His problem is that he will not compromise and bend his principles, not even to save his own community standing or reputation."

"I like a man with principles," Jessie said. "I think much more highly of attorney Adair now that you've explained to me his past circumstances."

"Good!" Pearl said, unable to hide her own disgust at the cockroaches on the floor. "And not only is Rollin the only man who will oppose the powers that be in Tucson, but he is the only attorney bright and educated enough to stand a chance against Richard Smith."

"Are you sure that he will take the case?"

"No," Pearl said. "He will only take the case if he believes in it. About the only cases he's handled these past few years, since he was almost tarred and feathered for his stance against the town, have been for the Mexican people. Little things like chicken stealing and so forth. But something like this . . . well, I just don't know. You see, Jessie, money is not Rollin's primary motivator."

"Obviously," Jessie said.

They heard him coming down the stairs, and when Jessie looked up, she saw a scholarly-looking man in his late twenties with wire-rimmed glasses, light brown hair and mustache, and piercing blue eyes. His features were quite prominent. He had high cheekbones and a broad, intelligent brow. He was quite handsome, in an aristocratic way, and when he looked at Jessie, his smile made him suddenly look young.

"So, Miss Starbuck," he said, "what an honor, I have long read about you and your father. I regret deeply that I never had the pleasure of meeting him."

Rollin Adair glanced around the room. "Please forgive the shabby circumstances of my accommodations. Principle, it seems, walks hand in hand through this world with poverty."

"Not necessesarily," Jessie corrected. "My father, as I'm sure you are aware, was a man of immense principle. And no one could say he died in poverty."

"I stand corrected. Although, one could argue that his poverty was in the few number of years he was allowed on this earth because of his principles."

"Yes," Jessie said with a smile of appreciation, "in that sense, you are correct."

Pearl smiled. "Rollin, we appreciate your willingness to meet with us at this last moment."

"I could do nothing less. Besides," Adair said, "I am broke and without a cause at the moment. And I hear that you have a good one for a man of my inclinations and talents."

Jessie resumed her seat on the worn hotel lobby couch. In as few words as possible, she told the attorney about Ki and Ricardo.

"So," Adair said, "at last we are about to apply some tarnish on the shiny facade of Mr. Smith's reputation."

"Yes," Jessie said. "I met with Ricardo's mother. She drew pictures of Richard Smith, and they are of such a great likeness that no one could mistake them."

"The boy has those pictures with him?"

"He does."

Adair frowned. "Miss Starbuck, I regret to say that the pictures, no matter how great the likeness, will not help us win a case or even exonerate Ki or Ricardo in court."

"But why not?"

"Because the woman could have seen the man in El Paso and simply sketched his likeness. They fail to prove the man is Ricardo's real father."

"Yes," Jessie conceded, "I understand. But that being the case, what can we do?"

"We can do little more than present the heartrending evidence of a boy who believes with all his heart that Richard Smith is his true father, who had promised to marry his mother and support her through good times and bad. And, when Smith cruelly denied any responsibility, then who could blame the boy or his friend, Ki, from erupting in righteous anger?"

"That's the best that we can do?" Pearl asked.

"The very best. And frankly, since neither are white, sympathy will be very hard to evoke."

Jessie's spirits sank. "The sheriff says that Mr. Smith is Judge Potter's son-in-law."

"That is true. But it is a marriage in name only. Mrs. Smith moved to California five or six years ago."

"Then perhaps the judge will be impartial."

"Not a chance," Adair said. "Judge Potter is an old rumpot who is counting on his son-in-law to support him from the bench. He wants very much for Smith to be appointed a judge. You see, a corrupt judge in this territory can make a lot of money. Potter certainly has. He would be a wealthy man if he were smart with money and not a common drunk who squanders his bribes on whores and whiskey."

Jessie shook her head. "Then tomorrow we can do nothing but plead for mercy?"

"We can try to strike a deal," Adair said.

"What kind?"

"The publicity surrounding an illegitimate child could be very damaging to Richard Smith and his political ambitions despite the fact that many voters somehow feel that there is nothing immoral about a married man having a Mexican mistress."

Jessie said nothing, because, unfortunately, Adair was correct in that blunt assessment.

"Even so," Adair continued, "the case has an element of sensationalism about it that would work against Smith's political future."

"So you're saying that some voters will overlook marital infidelity but not irresponsibility toward their illegitimate offspring, even if they are half-Mexican."

"Exactly so."

"Then you will . . . what?" Pearl blurted.

101

"I will seek to work out an out-of-court settlement that will free the boy."

"What about Ki?"

"A short jail term," Adair said. "No Yuma Prison."

"And Austin?"

Adair frowned. "He was very foolish to strike that deputy. But that should not be a prison term. Perhaps ten days to two weeks in jail and a fine."

"Go to work on the fine and as short jail sentences for Ki and Austin as possible," Jessie requested, realizing that everything Adair had said was true and that poor Ki and Austin would have to serve some time for assault.

Rollin Adair stood up. "I need to consult some of my law books so that I can speak to Smith in the morning and work a deal."

"You haven't said anything about a retainer or your fees," Jessie said.

"I know you are a very rich woman," Adair said. "But you know that I am a man of great principle. Why don't we see what happens and then let us talk about money?"

"All right," Jessie said with a shake of her pretty head. She stuck out her hand. "You are a very unusual man, Mr. Adair."

"And you are a very unusual woman," he said, then added, "like Miss Appleton."

Rollin Adair left them then and went back upstairs, his face already appearing distracted by the mental problems he would encounter when he confronted his adversaries in tomorrow's courtroom.

"Well," Pearl said, "what do you think?"

"I like and admire him very much," Jessie said. "But I'll reserve judgment until tomorrow when the sentence is handed down."

● ● ●

The next morning at precisely ten o'clock, Judge J. Potter banged his gavel down hard in the Tucson Municipal Courthouse, and the bailiff intoned, "Hear ye, hear ye, court is now in session, the Honorable Judge J. Potter presiding."

Jessie, along with a packed audience, stood and repeated the Pledge of Allegiance to the United States of America. That finished, everyone sat down and leaned forward with anticipation.

Judge Potter glared from his seat on the bench. He was dressed in a black robe with purple piping and a white collar, and that alone should have given him a dignified bearing, but it did not. The man, Jessie decided, just had a dissipated, dissolute look about him. His hair was uncut and greasy, and his eyes were bloodshot from drinking. He wore spectacles that kept sliding down his long, sloping nose, bulbous and red from burst vessels, and his undercut chin, coupled with his other features, gave one the overall impression of weakness.

"Let's try the first prisoner," he said to the bailiff. "Bring in the Mexican boy who calls himself Ricardo Smith."

It broke Jessie's heart to see Ricardo's wrists shackled with handcuffs. His head was held high, and when he passed his father, who had, for obvious reasons, excluded himself from being the prosecuting attorney, Ricardo lunged at the man.

The boy's attack was so sudden and unexpected that it caught the bailiff, who had been leading him, along with everyone else, by complete surprise. Ricardo struck his manacled wrists downward and caught Richard Smith across the bridge of the nose.

Smith howled with pain and reeled backward as Ricardo tried to rake his father's face again but was jerked backward and thrown to the floor. The judge pounded his gavel furiously and the courtroom erupted in chaos.

Jessie could do nothing but sit and watch helplessly as Ricardo was dragged up before the judge, who was yelling at him while banging his gavel.

When order finally was restored, Richard Smith was clutching a broken nose in his hands and there was blood in his handkerchief.

Potter's long, dissipated face was livid with anger. "In all my years on the bench I have never seen anyone more deserving of prison. For this unprovoked attack alone, I sentence you to—"

"Hold it!" Adair stormed. "This boy hasn't had a trial yet or even been given a chance to state his reasons for attacking Mr. Smith."

"There are no acceptable reasons for such behavior," Potter declared loudly.

"Aren't there? What about abandonment of a father's responsibility to his children? What about promises made to a destitute woman from Juárez, Mexico, who has spent her best years in love with and fidelity to a man who promised to marry her even though he was already married!

"And what about . . ."

Richard Smith had forgotten about his nose and was waving wildly at the judge, who was now banging his gavel again.

"Your Honor!" Smith cried. "In respect for the boy's age, I refuse to press charges against him."

Rollin Adair grinned coldly. He turned to Smith and said, "How very benevolent of you, Mr. Smith, to drop a jail sentence in exchange for fifteen years worth of promises to a woman and your two illegitimate children."

The audience was buzzing, and Jessie could see Smith's face grow pale. It seemed very obvious that the man would suffer almost anything to keep Ricardo from taking the stand and telling everyone about his family living in a hovel just south of the Rio Grande.

Judge Potter, for all his insensitivity, must have read the same look because he banged his gavel again and yelled, "As there are no charges, there can be no trail. Case dismissed!"

Ricardo did not understand. He had probably spent the whole night wrestling the idea of having to stand before a crowd and reveal his pain and disappointment as well as that of his poor mother. And now, he was to be shunted out the door, dismissed as if he were simply a common urchin of the street.

"But Señor Judge!" he cried. "I am not here for myself! I am here for justice for my mother!"

"Get him out of here!" the judge shouted. The bailiff hustled Ricardo out the door, and it hurt Jessie deeply to see the boy's face. Later, when the issue of Ki and Austin had been settled, she would go out and try to calm Ricardo down and explain things—if that were possible.

"Bailiff," Potter demanded, "bring in Mr. Peter Sedge Austin."

Jessie leaned over to Pearl and whispered, "Rollin was able to get a light jail sentence for Austin."

"Good," Pearl said with relief. "He is such a nice young man."

"Yes," Jessie said, thinking that she might have caught the glimmer of something special in Pearl's eyes when she spoke of the ex-stagecoach guard.

"The charge against you, Mr. Austin, is assault of a law officer. How do you plead?"

Austin took a deep breath. "Guilty as charged."

"Mr. Adair, your client pleads guilty. Will you defer to the mercy of this court?"

"Yes, Your Honor, I will do so."

Judge Potter slammed his gavel down hard. "Then I sentence this man to one week in jail for assaulting Deputy McDonald."

The courtroom was caught off-guard by this swift administration of justice. There were those who had expected each trail to take at least a day, possibly much longer. But now, two of the three prisoners had been sentenced and the court had not been in session more than twenty minutes. Judge Potter, who had never been known as a very decisive man, was in danger of changing his entire image.

"Bailiff, bring in the Chinaman."

"He's not a Chinaman at all," Pearl whispered angrily to Jessie.

"Of course not," Jessie said. "But to the ignorant, there is no distinction."

When Ki was brought handcuffed into the courtroom, Jessie's impulse was to jump up and race to his side and tell him that a deal had been struck between her attorney and Richard Smith. In exchange for the same short jail sentence that had been imposed upon Austin, Ki was to plead guilty to aggravated assault. Keeping a man like Ki in a cell for a week was a terrible punishment, but Jessie would do everything in her considerable power to make sure that he had everything possible to make his as well as Austin's stay as comfortable as possible.

"Mr. Ki," Judge Potter said in a solemn tone, "you are accused of aggravated assault. How do you plead?"

Ki said nothing but only glared at the judge.

Potter quickly grew angry. "Mr. Adair, are you representing this man?"

"I am."

"Then since he will not speak, you must do so for him. How do you plead?"

"Guilty as charged."

Potter's eyes narrowed as he gazed imperiously down at Ki. "Aggravated assault against a respected citizen of this city carries a heavy, heavy burden of guilt, mister. I sentence you to ten years in the Yuma Territorial Prison."

"What!" Jessie screamed as she jumped to her feet.

"Your Honor!" Rollin Adair shouted above the mayhem and noise created by the audience. "I protest! This sentence is outrageous. I move for a new trail."

"Your motion is denied!"

"Then we will appeal this sentence to the territorial governor!"

"He has already been consulted and approves of it!" Richard Smith snorted through his broken nose.

Through it all, the only one that remained calm and unemotional was the samurai. He stood quietly until the bailiff grabbed his arm and roughly led him out of the courtroom.

"We've been framed," Jessie said, collapsing in her seat as Pearl shook her head bitterly and grabbed Jessie's arm. "I don't know if Rollin Adair is in on it and is just putting on an act, or if he is sincere and has been double crossed."

"He would never do this to us," Pearl said.

Jessie, looking out at their attorney and seeing him so angry that he had to be physically restrained from attacking Judge J. Potter, knew that Pearl was right. They had been betrayed by Richard Smith and his father-in-law and even the territorial governor.

"What are we going to do!" Pearl wailed.

"We'll wait until Austin is out of jail, then we'll go to Yuma and help Ki escape," Jessie said.

"No one escapes Yuma Prison."

"Ki will," Jessie vowed. "And besides all that, we still have the issue of your father's murderer and the people who are trying to extort money from you under a death threat."

Pearl nodded her head. "With Ki in prison, I suddenly feel vulnerable," Pearl said. "I know what he can do, and without him. . . ."

"I understand," Jessie said, watching the samurai being led out of the court in shackles. "Believe me, I understand."

★

Chapter 12

As soon as the court was adjourned, Jessie helped Pearl outside, where they met the young Harvard attorney. Taking the man's arm and guiding him away from the crowd, Jessie said., "What went wrong?"

"The judge sold us out," Adair said with agitation. "I was promised that if we did not publicize Ricardo's situation, then Ki would receive only a very light jail sentence. I guess the judge felt that I said too much in his courtroom."

"That's obvious. So what can be done to change things?"

"Absolutely nothing. If a good man were appointed to replace Judge Appleton on the bench, we'd have a chance of overturning the conviction and most certainly of getting the sentence changed."

"But if Richard Smith is appointed," Jessie said, "then we're sunk."

"That's right."

"So who decides the appointment?"

Adair scratched the earth with the toe of his boot. "You're not going to want to hear this, Miss Starbuck."

"Let me take a guess. The governor, right?"

"I'm afraid so."

"Then we most certainly are in deep, deep trouble," Jessie said with a shake of her head, "because the governor and Richard Smith are in bed together."

"I couldn't have described it any better," Adair said. "I'm afraid we have to resign ourselves to the fact that we saved two out of three from prison."

"That's not good enough," Jessie said, "not even close. Ki means more to me than a best friend. He's saved my life many times. I won't let him rot for ten years in that hell-hole of a Yuma Prison. If we can't change that outrageous sentence, then I'll figure out a way of busting him free."

"Not much chance of that," Adair said. "Have you ever seen the prison?"

"No."

"Well, I have. Many times. It's on a bluff overlooking the Colorado River. It's surrounded by smooth rock walls that are more than five feet thick at the base and a good twenty feet high. And the lock-up cells are also made out of quarried granite. The cells are about ten by ten, each with two iron bunks three-tiers high. There's a guardhouse that overlooks the entire compound, and guards with rifles are ever alert. Escape is impossible."

"Not for a *Ninja*," Jessie said with conviction.

"A what?"

"Never mind. Let's just say that Ki could escape a buried coffin if he really wanted to."

Rollin Adair looked at her oddly but did not argue. Instead he brought up another matter that weighed heavily on his mind. "As for a legal fee, since I have failed you there is no charge, Miss Starbuck."

"Not by a long shot," Jessie said. "You had no choice but to play for the jury's sympathy when the time came for sentencing Ricardo. Had you not done so, Judge Potter would also have sent the boy to prison and that would have been a tragedy."

"I agree," Adair said. "I get the impression that your Ki is a man who can take care of himself."

"There are none better."

"Yes, well, little Ricardo, despite obviously being quite brave, would not have stood a chance against some of the murderers, rapists, and hardened criminals he'd have encountered in Yuma Prison."

Pearl joined them. She wasn't smiling. "So what do we do now?" she asked.

"We go to my hotel room and talk about alternatives and how it might be possible to get Ki out of prison."

Pearl and the lawyer did not look very hopeful, but Jessie paid them no attention. All her life she had been handling problems, and to her way of thinking, this was just one more to be taken care of and the sooner the better.

But by early evening, Jessie had no solution in sight. "We have been talking in circles for more than six hours," she said with exasperation. "The trouble is, we don't know any of the facts. I need to see that prison to figure out how we can help Ki escape."

Jessie stood up and paced about the room. Finally, she stopped. "Rollin," she said, "you'll need to work on the legal angle from this end while I go to Yuma and wangle a visit into that prison."

"Aren't you going to wait until Austin is out of jail?" the lawyer asked.

Even Pearl protested. "I really wish you would wait. Besides, how will you get to Yuma?"

"On horseback. I've got Sun, and it can't be much more than a couple hundred miles."

"But it's across the Sonoran Desert, and the heat will be terrible."

"I have to go," Jessie said. "If I can find an Army patrol or a wagon train to join, well and good, but if not, then I'll go alone."

"I don't like it," Adair said. "I'm working for you, but I have to say that I think leaving on your own is a bad mistake."

"I make them sometimes," Jessie admitted.

"But this one might be fatal."

Jessie shook her head. "I've already talked to several people. The Apache are raiding to the east of Tucson, not to the west. The road is well traveled, and I feel confident that I will be fine."

"When Austin hears about this, he'll go crazy," Pearl said.

"I can't help that," Jessie decided. "I owe far too much to Ki to wait even a single day. So if Austin wants to join me in Yuma, I could use his help. But I'd go crazy knowing Ki was in prison while I cool my heels waiting for Austin to be released from jail." She frowned. "I've got to find some way to get inside that prison and see Ki. Do they allow the prisoners to have visitors?"

"Only their immediate family on Sundays," the lawyer explained. "They're worried about weapons being smuggled in during visiting hours. They search everyone who comes to visit."

"I'll submit to a search if I have to," Jessie said, thinking how, by leaving tomorrow morning, she could be in Yuma on Saturday and see Ki the following day. "A search won't bother me."

"I don't think you'd like it," Adair warned, studying Jessie's voluptuous figure. "I'm afraid, given the way you look, the search would be more than thorough."

Despite the circumstances, Jessie had to grin. "I understand what you're trying to tell me," she said. "But surely they must have women to search women."

"Maybe," Adair said, "I don't know. But I'd say there was a very good likelihood that a woman like you would deserve special attention."

Jessie certainly did not relish the thought of some sweaty prison guard pawing over her person, but there might be little choice.

"There's also another little problem," Pearl said. "You don't look related to Ki's family."

"I could pose as his wife."

Pearl looked very dubious, and Jessie supposed that she could see her point. "I'll dye my hair and eyebrows black and do something a little Oriental-looking with my hair. I'm sure that I can pass for Ki's wife."

"What about poor Ricardo?" Pearl asked.

Jessie shrugged. "He needs some cheering up, and as soon as the stages are safely moving between here and El Paso, he should go home. There's nothing that can be gained from this end with his father. I'm afraid the man has hurt him very deeply."

"At least he paid with a broken nose," Pearl said.

Jessie had to smile. "Yes, at least he did that."

"When are you leaving for Yuma?" Adair asked.

"I'd leave tomorrow morning except that I'm worried about Pearl."

"Why?"

When Jessie explained about the threats on her life and the letter demanding money, Rollin Adair grew very upset. "Miss Appleton, I had no idea!"

"How could you?" she asked. "I don't think anyone would be in the habit of making a death threat public knowledge."

"And you've no idea who . . ."

"No," she said, "I don't."

Adair smoothed his mustache. "I don't wish to point fingers, but it seems only logical that the one who stands to profit the most from your father's death is our own Richard Smith."

"That's true," Pearl said. "And he was the first one that came to mind. However, why would he also demand extortion money? He's quite well off."

"He's not a stupid man," Jessie said. "Perhaps the extortion threat is merely a smoke screen to divert attention from himself, the most obvious suspect."

"Yes," Adair said. "That would be both clever and the sort of cunning thing that Richard Smith is known for."

Jessie left Pearl and Rollin Adair and went to find Ricardo. The boy was brushing his horse in a corral behind the livery and talking to the animal in Spanish.

"Ricardo?"

"*Sí?*"

Jessie slipped through the pole corral fence and walked over to the boy's horse. "I am leaving for Yuma in the morning. I may not see you for quite some time."

"I will go with you."

"No," Jessie said. "You are needed at your mother's side back in El Paso. I'm also sure that your little sister misses you very much."

Ricardo returned to brushing his horse.

"Ricardo, I know that you are angry and feel betrayed by your father. There is nothing I can say to make you feel any better about that. But you are a man now, and that means you have to learn to accept great disappointments. All your life, people will fail you, but you must not become bitter."

"I heard you speak many times about your father," Ricardo said, unable to meet her eyes. "He did not disappoint you."

"Not in the things that counted," Jessie admitted. "But in the small things, he could be very difficult and demanding. A man does not become rich by patting people on the back and smiling. No, my father was a hard taskmaster. He had many enemies. His temper was quick and he was very impatient with me, but even more with himself. Everyone has faults, Ricardo."

"My father betrayed my mother, my sister, and myself," Ricardo said. "He is ashamed of us."

Jessie touched the boy's shoulder. "He is foolish and more ashamed of himself, deep inside. You see, no matter how much money he has, it won't erase the fact that he failed his own son."

"When I am a man, I will never fail my woman. And when I have children, I will never leave them."

"And that is the way it should be." Jessie smoothed the horse's coat with her hand. "This is a good animal. When it is safe to leave for El Paso, have the stage tie him on a line so that he follows. I will leave you plenty of money for your ticket and the extra for this horse's feed. There will be even more money waiting for you and your family in El Paso."

"We cannot accept so much."

"Then bring your mother and sister to my Circle Star Ranch in Texas," Jessie said. "My foreman's name is Ed Wright. He will help you and your family in my absence. I will write a letter this evening asking him to help and then teach you to become a cowboy."

"I would rather be a vaquero, Señorita Starbuck."

"Good! I employ at least a dozen of them and they will teach you their skills with a reata."

Ricardo kept brushing his horse. "I still want to go to Yuma with you," he said. "You might need help."

"I will have Austin."

"He is a good man. Not as good as Ki, but a good man."

"That is true."

"Can you free Ki from the prison?"

"I think so."

Ricardo was silent for a moment before he said, "I have heard the prison is very bad in Yuma. That it is not fit for dogs."

"I've heard the same thing."

"I hope that he can get away quickly," Ricardo said. "And I wish that I could help you."

"You can," Jessie said. "As you know, Miss Appleton's life has been threatened. I want you to help Mr. Adair watch out for her safety."

"I cannot shoot very straight," Ricardo said, "but I would try." Jessie said, "Come with me now and I will buy you a good pistol. I think, given that you are still not fully grown, a nice Colt double-action .38 revolver would be just the ticket. It's much lighter than a Colt .45, but it will certainly do the job in a hurry if you are ever in trouble. I'll also buy you several thousand rounds of ammunition so you can ride your horse out to the edge of town and practice shooting until you are the equal of any man."

Ricardo's depression lifted instantly, and he was smiling when he fell in beside Jessie and headed for the nearest gun shop. Not that a new pistol would erase the pain he felt

116

inside at the betrayal of his father, but it would certainly help chase the blues away.

That night, when everything was in order and Jessie was ready to depart early the following morning, she found that she could not sleep. For more than an hour she lay on her hotel bed thinking about everything that had happened and wondering how everything would turn out for all of them.

At midnight, she climbed out of bed with exasperation. "To hell with it," she told herself. "Why wait until morning?"

Happy to be up and moving instead of fighting for sleep, Jessie quickly dressed and then grabbed her saddlebags. It would be better to leave tonight anyway, so that no one would realize she had gone.

The liveryman was none too pleased about her impromtu decision, but a few dollars extra turned his scowl into a sleepy smile. And so, less than an hour after giving up the quest for sleep, Jessie was swinging into her saddle and heading up the street. As she passed the sheriff's office, however, she impulsively reined her palomino over and tied it to the hitch rail. She strode up to the door and knocked on it loudly.

Her knock brought a sleepy-looking deputy to the door. He recognized her at once. "What do you want at this hour, Miss Starbuck? I ain't supposed to let anyone in after five o'clock."

"I need to visit Mr. Austin."

"You'll have to wait until tomorrow morning. I can't let you—"

Jessie dug twenty dollars out of her tight-fitting jeans. "I need to talk to him in private for an hour. No one will know."

117

The deputy, who probably did not earn more than twenty dollars in an entire month, swallowed. "I could lose my job."

"Why would either of us tell the sheriff of this visit?"

"But you might try to help the prisoner escape."

"You can search me for a gun and then lock us inside for an hour. When you return, I'll go and you can have your money."

The deputy was waking up fast. He grabbed Jessie's hand and pulled her inside. "Ten now, ten after."

"All right," Jessie said. "One hour. No more, no less."

The guard nodded eagerly.

"What the hell is going on?" a sleepy Austin said, rolling off the wooden bunk and its thin mattress, then rubbing his eyes and staring across the dim interior of the sheriff's office.

"I came to say good-bye," Jessie said.

Austin blinked and Jessie froze as the deputy removed her side arm, then moved his hands all over her body, lingering in all the wrong places. The search lasted only twenty or thirty seconds, but the deputy got his money's worth and then some. His touch made Jessie shiver with revulsion.

"My oh my," the deputy said, his eyes bright with desire, "you got a body that—"

"Lock me up and get out of here!" Jessie said harshly.

"First the money. There's a little whorehouse just around the corner, and I reckon that you gave me the need."

Jessie gave the man ten dollars and then waited until the deputy had drawn his own gun. "Austin, you get back against the wall."

"What the hell is going on here!"

"You got a paying guest," the deputy said with a wide smile. "I guess we both got lucky tonight."

A moment later, Jessie was shoved inside and the heavy steel door was locked behind her.

"Have fun!" the deputy called as he rushed for the door. "I sure as hell will."

When the office door banged shut behind him, Jessie turned to look at Austin who was still staring at her as if he could not believe his eyes.

"What are you doing this for?"

"I needed to say good-bye," Jessie said.

"Good-bye? Where are you going?"

"I'm riding for Yuma tonight."

"You can't do that! Not alone."

"I'm going," Jessie said. "But before I do, I wanted to make love to you."

"Holy cow!" Austin grated, reaching for her. "You are one crazy lady."

Jessie rushed into Austin's powerful arms and tasted his mouth. He fired her blood, and when he unbuttoned her blouse and his lips found her breasts, she felt a shiver pass all the way down to her toes.

"We don't have a lot of time," she said, "but let's make the most of it."

Austin undressed her quickly while her hands unbuttoned his pants and found his stiff manhood. Panting and kicking off their boots, they dropped down on the hard prison bunk and Austin raised himself over her.

"I bet nothing like this ever happened in this place," he panted.

Jessie spread her thighs and grabbed his manhood to guide it inside of her. She was hot and ready. "Come on," she whispered, "hurry!"

The big man was only too happy to oblige. He drove his thick root into Jessie, and she grunted with pleasure when his powerful hips began to thrust at hers.

"This is crazy," he groaned.

"It's also wonderful."

Jessie wrapped her long legs around his narrow hips and let him ride her hard. There wasn't much time, and the road to Yuma was also going to be long, hot, and very hard.

★

Chapter 13

The morning after being sentenced, Ki had been shackled hand and foot, then thrown in a prison wagon that very much resembled a tiger cage. Mercifully, the cage was six feet long and had a solid roof, so that in the hottest part of the day, when the sun was overhead, there was shade.

Three heavily armed guards had set out on the wagon across the blistering Sonoran Desert. The guards, having only the shade of their hats, suffered even more than Ki, and at night they were brutal.

"We ought to just kill the yellow bastard," a heavyset man said the very first night out on the trail. His name was Ernie and he had a beet-red face. "Then one of us could lay out his blanket inside that cage and travel like a king."

The other two guards nodded with weary agreement. "That'd be a fine idea," the one named Jim said, " 'cept you're forgettin' that we don't get paid unless we deliver our prisoners alive."

Ernie shook his sweaty head and mopped his brow with a muddy sleeve. "Goddammit, this is poor duty, boys. There sure as hell ought to be an easier way to make a livin' than hauling a Chinaman two hundred and twenty miles across the desert."

Jim frowned. "There's robbin' banks and stagecoaches. That's easy."

"It's also damned dangerous," the third man, named Hank, grumbled. "I *almost* robbed a stage once. It was just outside Silver City, New Mexico. Me and my three brothers got drunk and made up our minds to do 'er. You see, three stages in a row had been robbed on Seeger Grade. Sounded real easy to us."

"So what happened?"

"By the time we was able to sober up and get on our horses and get to Seeger Grade, the same gang robbed the stage again. Only this time, it was stuffed with United States marshals. They all had shotguns and blew them poor damned highwaymen and their horses all to hell. Next day, me and my brothers saw pieces of horse and highwayman hangin' off the sage and plastered to the rocks. It sure put the fear of Christ in us, I'll tell you."

"It would me, too," Jim said.

"Yeah, well, only a pack of loons would be stupid enough to rob the same stage four times in a row," Ernie said. "We ain't that stupid."

"There ain't no stages comin' anyway," Hank said. "Nothing but a couple freight wagons now and then."

"If it was the *right* freight," Ernie said, "could be worth the doin'. You know, if it was somethin' we could sell."

"Sell where? We couldn't go back to Tucson, and we sure as hell couldn't go to Yuma."

"Maybe we could take the loot south of the border and peddle it."

"For what!" Jim demanded. "A handful of tortillas and a pocketful of pesos? No thanks."

"Then how about tradin' it for Mexican cattle or horses?" Ernie said, stung by Jim's derision. "We could trade for horses or cows and drive them to some ranch or freighter and get hard cash. Nobody in this damned hard country is going to ask any questions."

"I think you're both crazy," Jim, the smallest and oldest of the three, said. "We each get ten dollars for delivering the Chinaman."

Hank and Ernie didn't look impressed. They looked hot and irritable as they poked at their fire and then laid back on their blankets and prepared to go to sleep.

"Hey!" Ki shouted. "How about some food and water?"

Hank sat up and glared at Ki. "You'll get some . . . about a mile this side of Yuma, if you last that long."

Ernie snickered. "He'll last. That one looks bigger and stronger than any Chinaboy I ever did see."

Ki glared at them. All day long he had thirsted and they had not given him a drop of water. Now, his tongue was already starting to swell and he was feeling a little sick.

"I need water," he repeated.

"I better give him a drink," Jim said, climbing to his feet and picking up a canteen. "We don't get paid for delivering corpses."

Hank and Ernie stared at him but said nothing as Jim passed the canteen through the bars, saying, "You drink it all now, you won't get anymore tomorrow morning."

Ki drank half the canteen. It wasn't as much as he wanted or needed, but it would do. "Obliged," he said.

"Did you really attack and beat the hell out of that lawyer?"

"I hit him, but only because he hurt his son. If I'd given him what he deserved, he'd be dead."

"I seen him swaggering up and down the streets of

Tucson. Lawyer Smith looks like the kind of snooty son of a bitch that needed to be taken down a notch or two. I kinda appreciate what you did for him, and from what I hear, he ain't much of a man."

Ki lowered his voice. "Neither are those two. You'd better not let them talk you into anything."

Jim smiled and started to laugh. "Here you are the jailbird tellin' me to be careful. Now that's rich!"

"Hey," Hank shouted, "what's so damn funny?"

Jim's smile died. "Nothin'," he said, taking back his canteen.

"You hear what I say," Ki repeated softly as the man started to turn away, "that pair will put you in the Yuma Prison alongside me."

"They're all talk," Jim said. "Nothin' but talk."

But two days later, Hank and Ernie were ready to do more than talk. They had overtaken a medicine wagon driven by an old drummer who wore a tall top hat, played a harmonica, and sold a medicinal brew called Dr. Root's Cure for the Ages.

"I'm Dr. Augustus H. Root, men!" the old drummer said, smiling widely. "And I tell you the truth, while I've got the medicine cure to keep me fit way past one hundred years, I was getting a might nervous and lonesome out here."

Hank studied the man's wagon and his two good horses. "Where you headed?"

"On my way to San Diego, I am! Going to stop at Fort Yuma and all places in between here and the blue Pacific Ocean. Going to cure the multitudes, I am! You boys look a little peeky me. Why, it just could be you need the cure."

"We don't need no cure for nothin'," Ernie growled. "We're healthy men. You got any liquor?"

124

"No sir!" Root twisted around on the seat of his wagon. He reached inside the box, where he no doubt lived and brewed his elixir, and produced a bottle. "Gentlemen, once you try my cure, you'll never again wish for common liquor. No sir!"

"Ha!" Hank snorted.

Root uncorked the bottle, upended it, and swallowed rapidly. As they watched, he drank the whole bottle, and it was quart-sized, too.

Smacking his lips, with his cheeks turning bright pink, Root hooted like a great horned owl and then tossed the empty over his shoulder. Ki heard it clink on a pile of other empties, and then the doctor produced another bottle. His eyes narrowing as if he were about to divulge some great secret, he whispered, "Boys, the first one is on me. The rest, a dollar a bottle, and you'll beg for more and feel better than you have since you were sweet sixteen."

Despite the heat, dust, and a hot wind, the three guards had to grin at Root. Hank rode over and took the bottle. "Doctor," he said, "this had better be good stuff."

"Oh, it is, my friend! It is! I sold more than three hundred bottles in Tucson alone last week! I've sold thirty more since, and I'll be clean out by the time I leave Yuma."

"You sold three hundred bottles?" Ernie asked.

"I did."

Ki could almost read the two bigger guard's evil minds. Three hundred bottles translated into *three hundred dollars*. It did not take any mathematical whiz to make the calculation.

"Then maybe we better try some," Hank said with a wink at his partner.

Root was only too happy to oblige. "It'll be a comfort to have friends to journey with on to Yuma," he said as he reached for the bottles. "I talk to my horses and I talk to myself, but that will drive a man crazy over time."

Root produced four bottles. He wrapped his lines around his brake and hopped stiffly down to the road. "Here you go," he said, handing each of the three riders a full bottle. "If this doesn't cure what ails you, nothing in this world will."

"To health," Hank said.

"And wealth," Ernie added, grinning into his friend's eyes.

Jim said nothing. The drummer came to the prison wagon and stared at Ki. "Son," he said, "I don't hold nobody short for the color of their skin. Yellow, red, black, white, or brown, we all got our ailments. You got a dollar?"

"No."

The drummer uncorked the bottle, took a long swig, and then shoved the bottle through the bars to Ki. "Here you go, brother. Where you're headed, you'll need all the help you can get."

Ki took the bottle just because he did not know when he might get another drink of water. He acted as if he were drinking, but he really only wet his tongue. The cure-all was strong, and it tasted like whiskey, licorice, and maybe some brandy.

Dr. Root turned to Jim. "What did the prisoner do, kill some men? Ravage a good woman? What?"

"He whipped Richard Smith, a prominent lawyer in Tucson."

The drummer's eyes dilated. He turned back to Ki. "Young man, most lawyers I've met ought to be whipped. It's a sad day when they cage and then send a man to a hellhole like Yuma Prison for winnin' a fistfight. A sad day indeed."

126

Ki just nodded. The drummer was obviously a little drunk, but he was a decent human being demonstrating some compassion.

The medicine man turned back toward his wagon. "Well, boys, how do you like it?"

Hank and Ernie had slugged their bottles down like it was cool water. Jim, however, had barely taken a drink, and he looked nervous.

"I like it fine," Ernie said. "How about another?"

"Cost you a dollar."

"I got it," Ernie said, flipping the old drummer his empty.

"So do I," Hank said. He tossed his bottle up in the air so that the drummer had to lunge forward for it with outstretched hands. At the same moment that the old man caught the empty, Hank drew his six-gun and shattered the bottle with a shot.

The bottle exploded in the drummer's fists, and the bullet entered the old man's chest just below the heart, as glass sliced across his face.

Dr. Root tottered backward until he leaned against the wheel of his wagon. He looked up at Hank's smoking gun, and then his gray eyebrows arched in a question, and he said something that Ki would not soon forget.

"Mister, if . . . if you didn't want . . . want to pay, you could have had it . . . free!"

Root's eyes glazed, and then he slid down to the earth and rolled onto his face.

Hank and Ernie began to laugh, but Jim was outraged. "If you wanted his horses and money, we could have taken it without killing the old bastard! You didn't have to shoot him!"

But the two men weren't listening. Instead, they were

jumping off their horses and climbing into the wagon, whooping and hollering with glee, already buzzed by the quart of brew they'd swilled and sure that they'd soon have three hundred dollars in their fists.

Jim's face was white. He looked at Ki, and the samurai said very quietly, "I warned you. When you're caught, you'll hang along with them."

"What can I do!"

"You got a key to this cage, let me out. We can take them. It's the only chance you have."

But Jim shook his head violently. "They'd kill us both."

"You'll hang if we don't stop them. Hurry up!"

Jim was a follower, not a leader, and, desperate, he obeyed the samurai. In a moment, the cage was unlocked and Ki was reaching into his tunic, where he had carefully sewn three *shuriken* star blades.

"What the. . . ."

Jim never had a chance to finish his exclamation because at just that moment, he heard Ernie shout, "I found it! Oh, Lordy, look at the cash!"

Ernie shoved his head out of the wagon and waved the money. "Hey, Jim, how's this for—Hey, what the hell is the Chinaman doing out of there! Hey, I—"

Ki's arm shot forward, and the *shuriken* star blade flashed in the bright desert air. It struck Ernie in the throat, and money flew from his hand to shower downward as he strangled in his own blood.

Hank cursed and stuck his head and arm out, with a Colt clenched in his big fist. "What the—"

Ki's arm shot forward again, and a second star blade bit into flesh, and this time into skull. Ernie's gun exploded downward, and a bullet ricocheted off the iron rim of a wagon wheel. His eyes crossed upward, and then he swatted his head and collapsed over the seat.

Ki turned to Jim, and the third guard raised his pistol. "I don't want to kill you, mister, but if you don't drop to the dirt and put your hands behind your back, that's what I'll do."

"Why don't you just walk away from this?" Ki said.

"I can't. If I go back with them dead and you escaped, I'll be the scapegoat. You don't know how things work in these parts."

"I'm getting an idea that there's no justice."

"That's right," Jim said, cocking back the hammer of his gun. "Now get down like I say, or so help me God, I'll shoot you."

Ki took a deep breath and expelled it slowly. He knew that Jim wasn't bluffing, and he also knew that he didn't particularly want to kill the guard.

"All right."

Ki dropped to the ground. "Now cross your wrists behind your back."

Ki did as he was told, and Jim came up behind and tied his wrists together.

"I'm sorry as hell about this," Jim said, helping Ki to his feet. "But it's my neck if I don't deliver you to the Yuma Prison."

"I won't be there for long."

"That's what they all say. I'll promise you this much, I'll let the warden know that you killed Hank and Ernie after they shot the drummer. I'll tell him you acted in self-defense. Maybe they'll just commute your whole ten-year prison sentence."

"That would nice," Ki said.

"But you need to get back into the prison wagon. I *have* to bring you in."

"I understand. What are you going to do about the bodies?"

"I'll bring them along."

Ki shrugged. "They'll get ripe in this heat pretty fast."

Jim paled a little. "Then . . . then we'll have to bury them somehow."

"Good idea," Ki said, climbing into the prison wagon.

Jim managed to load the bodies himself, then he scrambled around picking up the poor drummer's money. And finally, he loaded all the full bottles of the doc's medicinal brew.

"You can drink all you want," Jim said, uncorking a bottle and extending it through the bars.

"No, thanks."

Jim shook his head and took a long series of shuddering gulps. "Suit yourself," he said, "but as for me, I'm going to get drunk as a damn loon."

"That won't change what happened here."

"I know, but it'll still make me feel better."

"Not tomorrow morning."

Jim took another drink. "Don't you go to worrying about my head, samurai. If I was you, I'd start worrying about how I was going to survive ten years in the Yuma hellhole."

★

Chapter 14

The military outpost of Fort Yuma was on the California side of the Colorado River, and the Yuma Prison was on the Arizona side. Each facility was bleak and sun-blasted, surrounded by low, barren hills. By the time that Jim finally drove the wagon up to the gates of the prison, he was drunk and had stayed that way for more than fifty miles.

"Damn," he said brokenly, swaying on the wagon seat, "I sure do hate to do this to you, Mr. Ki. But like I said, it's either my ass or yours, and I'd sure rather it was yours."

"I can understand that," Ki said, all of his attention focused on the prison just ahead.

By craning his neck, Ki could get a very good view of the entire facility. The prison walls were constructed of rock smoothed over by adobe. They appeared to be very thick, perhaps as much as eight or ten feet at the base, but gradually narrowed to a five-or six-foot walkway about eighteen feet above the ground.

"You see that main guard tower?" Jim asked.

"How could anyone miss it?"

"It's manned by a Lowell battery gun, a four-muzzled weapon that can fire bullets faster than a Gatling gun. From where it's bolted, it has the ability to cover the entire prison compound. There isn't a spot except directly under it that can't be sprayed by bullets."

Ki said nothing. He had no intention of attempting to escape by throwing himself at the walls.

"And there are guards constantly patroling the catwalks on top the walls. A man would have to be crazy to try and escape during the daytime. And at night, he's locked in cells like . . . Well, I'm afraid you'll find out quick enough what the cells are like. The point of it is, you can't escape."

"So it would seem."

"But you're still going to try, ain't you?" Jim asked, twisting around in his seat to peer at the samurai.

"Yes."

"Listen, if you could last five years, you might get a pardon," Jim said, almost pleading. "Most prisoners serve only about half their sentence if they behave."

"I'd never last five years," Ki said. "It would kill my spirit."

"Better your spirit than your body."

"I don't think so," Ki said as they approached the main gate and the tower guards wheeled the big battery gun around to cover the prison wagon.

"Open the gate!" Jim called, yanking off his hat and waving it around so that the men above could recognize him.

"What happened to Hank and Ernie?" a guard demanded.

"It's a long story. Too damn long to tell out in the sun."

"You drunk?"

"Yeah. But I got plenty more liquor to share."

"Well, don't tell that to the warden, for crying out loud," the guard said before yelling to another man to open the gate.

The gate swung open and the prison wagon rolled inside. It was immediately surrounded by guards with grim expressions and shotguns and rifles.

"What's this one here for?"

"Assault. Ten years."

"Ten years!" a guard exclaimed with disbelief. "Who'd he assault, the governor?"

"Nope. Attorney Richard Smith, Judge Potter's son-in-law."

"Well that's damn near as bad."

Jim tried to climb down from the wagon, but he hooked his toe on the wheel and crashed headfirst into the dirt.

"He's sotted. Throw him in that horse water trough!" a big, pot-bellied man, with a shiny badge on his chest, ordered.

The man stepped over to unlock the door to Ki's cell. "Chinaman, I want you to raise your hands, and don't you so much as blink when you climb out of this wagon."

"I'm not a Chinaman," Ki said. "I'm a samurai."

"You're a prisoner," the man spat, "and my name is Mr. Bill Haney. I'm assistant warden here under Warden Pitney. When I say you jump, you better better jump tall and stay up in the air until I say you can drop, or your ass is gonna get pounded. Is that understood?"

Ki stared at the assistant warden, and then he glared at the guards who had their weapons trained on him. "Yeah."

Haney jammed his forefinger into Ki's chest. "Don't you ever 'yeah' me, Chinaboy! It's 'Yes, sir' to your kind of maggot! Understand!"

Ki nodded even though he wanted to drive his foot into Haney's testicles and ruin him for the rest of his life.

"Get him into the receiving cell and get him processed," Haney shouted to one of his subordinates. "Right now, I'll get Jim sobered up and cleaned up before he sees the warden. He's going to have a lot of explaining to do before the day is out."

Ki could see a pair of the guards driving Jim's face in and out of the water trough, sometimes holding it under until the man was thrashing wildly for breath. This, the samurai reasoned, was not going to be a nice place to visit.

"All right, prisoner, let's go," Haney said, prodding Ki forward.

They entered the prison through a pair of massive, strap-iron grilled gates, which swung beneath a thick archway. Inside, Ki realized that the walls were even a little taller than he'd imagined, were made primarily of adobe brick, and were nearly ten feet thick. When he glanced upward, he saw a grizzled old guard staring down at him with a 44–40 Winchester rifle clutched in his bony talons.

"That's old Art Case," the assistant warden said. "He's one of the finest marksmen in the Arizona Territory. He's probably noticing what you're looking at and just hoping you think you can escape. Old Art, now he'd like nothing better than to put a big slug through your heart. He just prays for a chance to prove he's still the best with that rifle."

Ki noted Art's intense, hawklike eyes and the thin, cruel cut of his mouth. "I'll just bet he does," Ki said. "And—"

The samurai never finished what he had started to say because Haney laced his fingers together and brought his fists crashing down against the base of Ki's neck. Ki's knees buckled and he collapsed in the prison yard. A blinding pain radiated out to his extremities, and he tried to rise to his feet, but the big assistant warden booted him in the ribs.

"Uggh!" Ki grunted, rolling away to avoid another kick aimed at the opposite set of ribs.

Haney's boot just grazed Ki under the arm, and before the fat man could regain his balance, Ki lashed out with his own foot and struck him against the side of his knee. Haney bellowed with pain, then tumbled to the dirt, clawing at the gun on his hip.

"No!" a man shouted.

The voice froze Bill Haney. He twisted around in the dirt to see Warden Walt Pitney come striding out of his office. The warden's face was contorted with anger. "What the hell is going on here!"

Haney was on his feet, but Ki's kick had done enough damage to his right knee that he wasn't about to put any weight on it.

"This new prisoner attacked me!" the assistant warden cried.

"The hell he did," Pitney snapped. "I saw what happened. How many times I got to tell you that I will not tolerate any unnecessary brutality!"

"But . . . but goddammit," Haney exploded, "he near to broke my knee!"

"Then you'd better get over to the dispensary," the warden said. "Have the doctor take a look at the damn thing. If it's broken, maybe I'll get a replacement for you yet."

Haney was blistered by his boss. Cursing and fussing, he limped off toward the dispensary.

"Prisoner, did he kick in any ribs?"

Ki pushed himself to his feet. His head was spinning as he ran his fingers over his ribs. "No, Mr. Pitney, I don't think he did."

"Warden," the man corrected. "You must always call me Warden. And as for what just happened, you might come to regret that I stepped in at all. You've made a very bad enemy."

Before Ki could think of anything to say to that, the warden turned away and headed back to his square adobe office.

"Let's go," a guard said, shoving Ki toward a low set of buildings. "You got any personal belongings?"

"No."

"The territory will issue you stripes, a toothbrush, comb, and a blanket, though it's hot enough here that you'll not want to use it for anything but a pillow. First though, inside."

Inside the small adobe building, Ki was forced to undress. His clothes were stuffed into a bag, and with his hands still cuffed behind his back, he was made to bath in a strong disinfectant, then led over to a rack of prison uniforms. All of them were striped, some vertically and some horizontally.

"Choose a pair that looks as if it fits," the guard ordered.

Ki found a pair that fit him in the chest but were a little too short in the leg and sleeve.

"They'll do," the guard said. "Ain't nobody gonna notice how pretty or ugly you look in this place."

Ki was then shoved into a barber's chair. The barber, a jovial, sweaty-faced man in his fifties, joked, "Well, Chinaman, I heard that you believe that if you lose your queue, you'll go to hell when you die. Is that right?"

"I wouldn't know. I'm Japanese and American."

"Humph!" the man grunted as he raised a big pair of shears, the kind that were used to shear sheep. "Well, never mind then. But when I finish with you, you'll have more hair on your ass than you will on your head."

The barber laughed at the comparison, and Ki ground his teeth as the man began to grab his long black hair and cut it off in great big hunks. The samurai could do nothing but sit still and endure the punishment, which was not made any more bearable by the fact that the shears were dull and had a tendency to pull rather than cut.

At the end of ten minutes, Ki was spun around in the chair to study his own relection in a cracked mirror. "Take a good look at yourself," the barber said. "It'll be the last you'll have until you're released."

The barber turned to the guard. "How long is this one in for?"

"Ten years."

The barber began to laugh uproariously, and that was when Ki judged the man to be crazy, or at least addled.

"Ten years!" the barber exclaimed. "Why, he won't last ten months!"

The guard, looking a little unnerved himself by the barber's hysteria, grabbed Ki by the arm and hustled him out the door and across the prison yard.

Ki noted how much attention he was receiving as he was prodded toward a cell. At least fifty convicts were staring at him, some out of curiosity, others with cold, calculating eyes. Ki glared at them all.

"Cell ten," the guard said, pulling Ki to a halt before a cell made of rock, with doors of heavy strap iron. "You got five men already living in here, prisoner. One bunk left on top. Whatever problems you have, save them for tomorrow. We don't interfere with what goes on in these cells at night.

137

That's between you and the other prisoners."

"Nothing will 'go on,'" Ki said contemptuously, for he understood what the guard meant.

"Maybe," the guard said, unlocking the heavy iron gate and swinging it open on rusty, prostesting hinges, "but being on that top bunk ain't going to save you."

In response, the samurai went over to the lowest of the three-tiered bunks. He grabbed a prisoner's blanket and tossed it up on the third tier, then threw his own blanket down.

"My oh my!" the guard said with a low whistle. "You are just bound and determined to get yourself killed tonight. I can see that right now. You'd better put that blanket back and climb on up to the top, or Big Al will stomp the other side of your ribs. And believe me, he can do a whole lot better job than the assistant warden. That much I promise."

Ki flopped down on the lower bunk. "You want to see Big Al fall," he said without a trace of brag in his voice, "just stick around."

The guard laughed as he locked the cell door and then walked away. And Ki, his ribs aching and his spirits never lower, stared up at the bottom of the bunk overhead and contemplated how long it might take him to escape this Yuma hellhole.

★

Chapter 15

It was late afternoon when Ki heard the guard at the tower shout, "open the gates for prisoner work detail."

The samurai had remained stretched out on Big Al's lower bunk. Alternately, he dozed and meditated, and after three hours, he felt much refreshed, although his ribs were still aching from the kick he'd received from the assistant warden.

He could hear the prisoners being marched across the prison yard as the iron gates protested being closed again. A moment later, a voice yelled, "Prisoners dismissed until chow!"

Ki heard an audible sigh from the men. He turned his head to see them come dragging back toward their cells, where they would rest or nap until suppertime. There was little conversation, and the men moved with great weariness. Some had chosen to wash away the sweat and the dust by taking a short plunge in the Colorado River while under the watchful eye of the guards. These men were still wet, but most of the prisoners had been too weary and still

139

remained covered by dried grit and grime.

"Hey!" a man exclaimed as they neared cell ten and could see inside its dim recesses. "Someone's sleeping on Big Al's bunk!"

Ki did not want to be caught lying down when Big Al found him, so he stretched his muscles, then rolled to his feet. He placed his hand on his injured ribs and reminded himself that it would be wise to avoid being hit or kicked there again in a fight.

"All right," a deep voice growled as Big Al filled the doorway. "I guess it's yellow-ass kicking time."

Ki eased back against the wall. "I'm a samurai," he said almost conversationally. "I think you'd better take the bunk on top."

The man was ape-like, with a lantern jaw, a thick overhang of brow, and a low forehead. His arms were too long for his body, and his legs were short, but thick as barrels. Al was shirtless and his torso was burned almost black by the sun, except for his chest, which was covered with a thick mat of curly gray hair. Ki judged the man to be in his early forties, though he might have been ten years younger but greatly aged by prison life.

Al stepped inside. "What are you in for?"

"Assault."

"You whipped a man?" Al asked, his voice dripping with contempt. "A damn runty little Chinaman."

"I'm a samurai," Ki repeated.

"You're meat," Al growled, advancing with his fingers splayed wide.

Ki set his feet on the hard-packed cell floor. Most men would ball their fists and come at you—this one had no intention of administering a beating—he was out to break his opponent's neck or throttle him to death.

140

Al lunged, and the samurai slipped under the much larger man's arms, driving his fist into Al's solar plexus so hard that the bigger man wheezed and grabbed his chest. Ki passed behind the man, driving the heel of his hand into Al's kidney area and causing him to straighten and gasp with pain.

To Ki's surprise, Al not only remained on his feet but spun around. "Goddamn you!" he shouted, rushing Ki, who had been backing toward the doorway.

A prisoner just outside the door to their cell kicked the samurai right behind the knees, driving him to the floor, and Al pounced on Ki like a cat on a mouse.

"Now I'm gonna scramble your brains out across the floor!" Al bellowed, landing astraddle Ki's chest.

Ki had other plans. His rigid fingers spiked upward and connected just under the apex of Al's jaw and throat. Al choked and released Ki for an instant, and the samurai caught his opponent just under the ear with a slice of his hand. Al rocked sideways, and Ki tried to throw the man off, but Al clamped his sides with his knees and managed to drive his fist into Ki's eye.

It was a wild, off-balance blow, but it stunned Ki for a moment. Bucking and twisting in a desperate attempt to free himself from Al's weight, Ki dimly heard the other prisoners shouting for their friend to finish the fight.

Al was trying. He grabbed Ki by both his ears and slammed his head down on the floor. Ki flung his legs up, hooked Al with his heels, and yanked him over backward. They rolled, each trying to be the first to get to his feet.

Ki was first, but he was still dazed. Al charged, and it was all the samurai could do to get out of the bigger man's way. Al crashed over Ki's outstretched leg and skidded out through the doorway, cursing and tearing the flesh from his hands, forearms, and elbows.

"Damn you!" Al screeched, climbing to his feet, whirling around and charging back inside.

Ki knew that he had to end the fight quickly. Al had taken some of his best hand strikes and was still on his feet. The samurai's left eye was swelling shut, and he knew that the back of his head was bleeding from where it had been mashed on the floor.

Ki tensed, and then he jumped up and delivered a perfectly timed and executed snap-kick to the much larger man's groin. He felt his foot crush Al's testicles as if they were grapes, and he saw Al's mouth fly open as a scream filled his throat.

"Ahhhh!"

Ki landed on his feet at exactly the same instant the heavily calloused edge of his right hand chopped down against Al's thick neck. The ape-like prisoner toppled like a tall tree, striking his forehead on the steel corner of his own bunk and opening up a huge gash on his forehead.

The prisoners stared at Ki with disbelief. Hardened men all, they could not quite comprehend that the slender young man before them had actually whipped Big Al. And whipped him badly.

"Someone better get this man over to the infirmary before he bleeds to death," Ki said to no one in particular.

Several of the inmates nearest the door exchanged nervous glances, unsure whether or not to enter.

"Come on!" Ki shouted, sitting heavily on Al's bunk. "Get him out of here!"

Three men, including the one that tripped Ki, jumped in, grabbed Al, and hauled him out the door.

142

Ki stretched out on the bunk and yawned, then closed his eyes. "Someone wake me when it's time to eat."

He actually did sleep, though not for long. Someone gently nudged his bunk and said, "Say, mister, it's time to eat."

Ki opened his eyes to regard a slight, intelligent-looking man in his early twenties, who was staring myopically at him through thick spectacles. "Thanks."

"It's all right," the man said. "I guess you got the whole damned prison talking about what you did to Big Al. They say he's pretty messed up. Balls are swelled to the size of grapefruit. The word is, he's going to find a knife and use it on you."

"He can try," Ki said, coming to his feet. "What's your name?"

"Elliot."

"What are you in here for?"

"I got drunk and stole some things from the general store. They caught me going out the back, and I got into a fight with the deputy who tried to arrest me. I was losing, so I bit off his little finger. The judge gave me two years."

"I got ten for doing a whole lot less," Ki said.

"I guess the severity of a man's sentence depends entirely on how the judge is feeling on the day you go into his courtroom," Elliot said. "You must have caught Judge Potter on one of his bad days."

"You mean he has good days?"

Elliot smiled. He wore thick, wire-rimmed glasses, and he had the appearance of an educated man. "Do you work on the detail outside this place?"

"Yeah," Elliot said. "It's called the chain gang, and in the summertime, the work will kill a strong man. I'm tryin' real hard to get a job in the warden's office. But hell, that's a job you have to buy, and I've got no money or connections."

"Maybe you'll get lucky," Ki said.

"Luck has nothing to do with getting off the chain gang. You either survive it, or you give up and die."

"Let's go eat."

"Follow me," Elliot said.

The chow hall where the prisoners ate was spartan. The inmates filed past a serving table where potatoes, beef, and a piece of boiled cabbage were dumped onto their tin plates. The choice of drink was water or coffee.

"Take the coffee," Elliot whispered. "It's still made out of muddy river water, but at least you can't see the dirt particles floating."

Ki took the coffee and followed Elliot to a table, all the time very aware that everyone was staring at him.

"Never mind," Elliot whispered, leaning across the table. "They'll get used to you in a few days. It's just that no one can quite believe you really whipped Big Al."

"I'll bet that they believe he will knife me, though."

"Oh yes," Elliot said, digging into his meal, "they're looking at you like they would a walking dead man."

"Great," Ki said. "I was planning to escape, but not for a day or two. I think maybe I better try tonight."

Elliot actually dropped his fork. "Are you crazy!" he hissed. "You can't escape this place."

"Oh yes I can. I'm *Ninja*."

"You're what?"

"In Japan, the *Ninja* are called 'invisible assassins,' and they are trained to sneak through all barriers to make their kill."

Elliot wasn't the least bit impressed. "You'd just be asking to get shot. Let me tell you this, if Assistant Warden Haney doesn't kill you, then Big Al will."

"So what do I have to lose by trying to escape?" Ki asked.

Elliot forked himself a big mouthful of potatoes. "Damned if I know. But if I had any money, I'd bet you one hundred to one that you won't even be able to get out of our cell."

"Yeah," Ki said, remembering the lock and the fact that all of his weapons were gone. "I might need a few days to find a wire or something to pick the lock."

"Even if you do," Elliot said, "you still wouldn't get over the walls."

Ki was hungry and began to eat. He was pleasantly surprised to find that the meal was very good. Better than some cafes and many stage stations where he and Jessica had been forced to dine.

When the prisoners finished their meal, they were lined up in the chow hall and searched for weapons or utensils and then marched out to their cells, where they were counted off before the doors were locked for the night.

Ki met his other four cellmates. They were deferential to him because of what he had done to Big Al, but they weren't a bit friendly.

"Lights out," a guard shouted as he marched past their cell. "It's nine o'clock and lights out."

Everyone blew out their candles, and the samurai lay down on his creaking bunk and gazed up at the sagging bunk just a foot over his head. He laced his fingers behind his head and thought about Jessie, Ricardo, and the death of Judge Appleton. The more Ki thought about it, the more it seemed pretty obvious that the man who had the most to gain from the judge's murder was none other than Richard Smith. Smith was the one that figured to be Appleton's replacement on the bench. It was Smith that was in cahoots with Judge Potter.

But how to get proof that Smith, maybe even Judge Potter, were responsible for the death of Judge Appleton as well as several other Arizona Territory judges.

It was long after midnight when Ki finally got up from his bunk and walked over to the strap-iron cell door and gripped it powerfully to test its setting. The door, as expected, was as solid as the rock upon which Ki stood. The samurai stared out through the strap-iron lattice and listened to prisoners snoring and, farther out, the mournful howling of a band of coyotes.

He could see the stars, brilliant pinpoints against the backdrop of inky sky, and he longed to walk away from his imprisonment and go out into the desert and simply be at peace. Never before had he been in such a foul, hard place as this. Being locked up was a trial to the soul. It made a man feel smaller both in body and in spirit.

"Hey," Elliot whispered, "what's wrong, can't you open the damn lock?"

"Not even a samurai can do that without a little help," Ki said quietly.

Elliot rolled out of his bunk and yawned. "I guess the first few nights a man is locked up he just feels like the walls and everything around him are leaning inward and they're going to crush him to death."

"Man wasn't meant to be locked up like this," Ki said.

"I hope, given that the assistant warden and Big Al both want to kill you, that you live long enough to get used to it."

Ki had to smile. "I'll be gone soon enough," he vowed. "I've some some pretty imporant things to do."

"Like what?"

Ki turned and studied the man's dark profile. "There's a lot of hard men in this place. Have you ever heard any of them mention anything about Arizona judges being murdered?"

There was a long silence, then, "Why do you ask?"

"A friend of mine, Judge Appleton, was murdered in Tucson a short while back. I hear that there are others who have died. I'd like to know why."

Elliot moved a little closer. "You're not a plant, are you?"

"If you mean someone that was put in here to find out things, then no," Ki said. "I really was sentenced to ten years."

"So if that's the case, why are you worrying about judges?"

"Because I don't intend to be in here very long, and I do intend to see that Judge Appleton's murderer is brought to justice."

Elliot was plenty wide awake now. "So what makes you think that someone in the Yuma Prison might know something?"

"I don't know," Ki admitted. "It's just that birds of a feather really do flock together. That, and the fact that the inmates in this place come from all over the territory. I just have a feeling someone in here might know something."

"Yeah," Elliot said. "So what's it worth to you?"

When Ki did not answer, Elliot said, "I mean, has the judge got some rich relatives or something that are willing to pay for the information? Nothing in this place comes free."

"There's money for information," Ki said. "You interested?"

"Hell yes! If you're for real. I mean, I'm not going to stick my neck out looking for trouble without some assurance that I stand to gain something."

"How about money and an immediate release?"

Elliot snickered in the darkness. "Sure, and maybe you could throw in a willing woman and a couple of bottles of French champagne."

"Anything is possible," Ki said.

Elliot stared at him for several moments before he said, "You're really serious."

"That's right."

"Look," Elliot whispered, "let me ask around for a couple of days. If I find out something and you're still alive, then maybe we can do some business. Okay?"

"Sure," Ki said.

Elliot shook his head. "I'd think you were an honest-to-God looney except that you said you were going to whip Big Al, and by damned, you did!"

"What I promise," the samurai said, "I usually find a way to deliver."

Elliot crawled back into the other lower bunk, opposite Ki's. "Let's get some sleep," he said. "Tomorrow is going to be another long, hot day in hell."

Ki nodded and slipped back into his bunk. Elliot was right. Ki just hoped the man was also able to get him some badly needed information about Judge Appleton's killer. It was a long shot, but it was the only one he had to play right now.

★

Chapter 16

Five o'clock came around in a great hurry as a guard marched past the cells, banging a metal pipe. "All right, all right! Everyone up and out of there! Roll call! Roll call!"

Ki climbed painfully to his feet. The previous day's fight with Big Al and the booting he'd received from the assistant warden, Bill Haney, caused the samurai to grit his teeth against his pain.

He must have also groaned, because Elliot said, "You should make sick call today and go to the dispensary. You're in no condition to go out on a road gang."

"I got a feeling it would be healthier to be outside these gates than inside," Ki said, thinking of Haney and Big Al.

"Yeah," Elliot said, reading the samurai's thoughts, "I suppose you're right. But it will be tough. We're building a road through Yuma, and it's hard pick and shovel work. The gang boss, he won't cut you any slack because of your ribs. In fact, he'll probably push you right to your limits."

Ki's eyes narrowed. "I will do what I have to in order to stay alive."

"Right," Elliot said. "And if I can help, I'll do it."

"Why?"

Elliot held his answer until the other four men in their cell had filed outside and started to line up for breakfast.

"Because I thought about what we talked about last night. Mister, I don't know who or what you are, but I got nothing to lose by helping you and a hell of a lot to gain."

"That's right," Ki said.

Elliot shoved a wide-brimmed cloth hat into Ki's hands. "Fold, then slip it between your belly and your pants," the man advised. "When we get out on the road, the guards will let you wear it. Without a hat, the sun will fry your brains and burn your face to a cinder."

"Thanks," Ki said, taking the hat and slipping it behind his waistband before he pulled on his shapeless black-and-gray striped prison jacket. With a guard yelling in his face, the samurai hurried outside to get into line.

The eastern sky was ablaze, and Ki overheard one prison guard say, "It'll be well over a hundred today. Gonna be a bitch out there."

"The hell with it," another guard replied. "I got a shade tree picked out. River's still close enough to cool off in, and I'm drawin' steady pay."

"Yeah," the other guard said as they walked away, "but I sure wouldn't want to be one of those poor bastards. Especially that Chinaman."

Ki didn't have time to worry about the implications of what he heard, because he was shoved into line and marched back into the chow hall. He passed through a serving line manned by sleepy, irritable prisoners who slapped the food on tin plates with wooden spoons.

Breakfast was porridge, toast, and strong black coffee. All a man wanted, and Ki wanted plenty. He figured that

150

he would be worked harder than he'd ever been worked in his life. No matter, he was in peak physical condition despite his aches and pains. The thing that had him most worried was the heat.

"You got to drink as much coffee as you can," Elliot whispered. "You'll sweat it out in a few hours, and your body will dry up fast."

Ki nodded and went for another cup of coffee, but a guard stopped him short. "You've had enough."

"I'd like more coffee."

"And I'd like you to give me some trouble, prisoner! That way, I could take my gun and put a hole in your head. How'd that be!"

Ki turned around, and the guard shoved him hard back toward his table. A few moments later another guard yelled, "Work detail! Road gang work detail!"

The trusty and most-favored inmates had jobs inside the prison. Some worked in the kitchen either cooking or washing dishes, pots and pans. Others labored in the laundry, and a few of the most fortunate were assigned the jobs of policing the grounds or helping in the warden's office.

Those prisoners that had no clout, money for bribes, or important outside connections were assigned to the road gangs. Ki, along with Elliot and most of the others, was marched out to the main sally port, then ordered to stand at attention while leg irons and chains were attached to the prisoners' right ankles. All linked together, they stood sweating in the sun.

Ki wondered what they were waiting for, until he saw the assistant warden emerge from his little office and sleeping quarters. Haney shoved his shirttail into his pants and then ran his fat fingers through his hair. Limping noticeably from the kick that the samurai had administered to the side of his knee, Haney made his way painfully over to the road gang.

The assistant warden passed by the shackled prisoners, inspecting each of the leg irons and making sure they were all locked. When he came to the samurai, he suddenly bent down and grabbed ahold of the shackle, then gave it a violent wrench.

Ki almost lost his balance and fell. He would have fallen if the prisoner next to him hadn't pushed him erect to keep from falling himself. Even so, the shackle cut into the flesh around Ki's ankle deep enough to draw blood.

"I guess it's on tight enough," Haney said, spitting his words into Ki's face. "But because you look like a damned runner to me, you're going to wear a ball and chain all day long, Chinaman. And you're gonna work twice as hard as any man on this gang. You understand me?"

"I understand that the day will come when we are both outside these walls."

Haney cursed and balled his fist, but one of the guards whispered, "Warden is watching!"

Haney did not look around to see the warden, but as he lowered his fist, he hissed, "I could have you killed quicker than you can bat your eye."

Haney's lips drew back from his teeth. "But I thought it all out, and instead, I'm gonna see that you are worked to death, nice and slow."

Before Ki could say anything more, Haney grabbed the samurai's prison jacket, lifted it up, and took away his hat.

"You won't be needing a hat today," Haney said with a smile as he squinted into the hot, rising sun. "It'd just slow you down."

Ki ground his teeth together in frustration. He had been taught, as a samurai, never to kill in rage, but only in self-defense or in defense of the person he had sworn to protect with his life. But right now, Assistant Warden Haney was testing him to his very limits.

Haney laughed, and then he turned and walked away.

"Detail, march!" the guard shouted as the gates were thrown open and the work gang was forced to march out of the prison and off down the hot, dusty road toward town.

Very quickly, Ki learned how to swing his shackled right leg in unison with the other prisoners. At first, it was a little awkward and he almost tripped on the chain, but it was something that came quickly to a man.

They marched for better than a mile through the dusty streets of Yuma, men, women, and children staring at them with looks ranging from fear to intense dislike. When they reached the eastern perimeter of town, they came upon a prison wagon and more guards waiting.

"Road gang, halt!"

The prisoners stopped shuffling and stood with bowed heads while their shackles and chains were removed.

"All right, boys," the guard said, "get your picks, pikes, and shovels and get to work. Before we quit this evening, we're going to widen this road another two hundred yards."

There was a low groan among the prisoners, and Ki could see why. The road was cobbled with big stones, and every foot of it had to be dug down about six inches, then smoothed and graded by hand.

"All right!" the guard repeated, "get your tools and get to work!"

Ki started to move toward the prison wagon, where the tools were being handed out under the watchful eye of several armed guards.

"Whoa, there!" said a big redheaded guard with a half-chewed cigar hanging out of the corner of his mouth, as he grabbed Ki's arm. "We got a little something extra for you, boy."

Ki turned his eyes away from the leering face as a ball and chain were snapped onto his ankle.

"*Now* you can get your tool," the guard said, shoving Ki toward the wagon.

The only tool left unclaimed was a five-foot-long steel pike, and when the samurai picked it up, he realized it must have weighed at least twenty-five pounds.

"Too bad," a guard said in a mocking voice. "The pike is for diggin' out the big rocks. It's the toughest job on the gang. Sorry."

Ki hoisted the pike and shuffled over to the road gang, which was already starting to work.

"Rock down low," an inmate intoned a few minutes later.

"Pike man!" a guard shouted at Ki. "Dig it out or bust it up."

Ki had never used a pike before, but it was such a primitive tool that no one had to tell him what to do. One end of the pike was sharp, the other hammered down to a short, thick blade. Ki drove the blade in next to the rock, lifted the pike, and drove it down.

The ground was flinty, but the heavy pike broke through the crust, and after ten minutes of hard slamming, Ki had the pike in far enough to lever the rock out of its cradle. By then, he was bathed in sweat and his chest was heaving.

"Slow down!" Elliot hissed. "You won't last half a day at that pace."

Ki sleeved his brow and nodded. Elliot was right. He had to pace himself, go as slow as the guards would allow, or he would not last.

All morning, the road gang grunted, sweated, and beat at the hard earth. The prisoners kept asking for water, and the guards, realizing that a man would dehydrate and go into seizures if not given copious amounts of water, gave them as much as they wanted.

By noon, the gang had widened the road a hundred yards. But they were exhausted, and when the guards called for a halt to eat, the prisoners staggered over and collapsed against a barn that offered them shade.

Several minutes later, trustees came by with more water, beef sandwiches, and apples. Ki was almost too tired to eat, but he knew that he had to try.

"You're still working too hard," Elliot whispered. "You can't last out the afternoon!"

"Watch me," Ki said, gulping water.

They were given just half an hour to eat and rest, then prodded to their feet again. By now, the temperature was well over one hundred and the sun was directly overhead. Without a hat, Ki felt as if his brain was slowly simmering in its own cranial juices.

"Pike man!" a guard shouted. "Big rock here!"

Dragging his ball and chain, which had chafed his ankle badly enough to draw blood, Ki shuffled over to his fallen pick. When he grabbed it, an involuntary cry escaped his lips and he dropped it.

"Ha!" the guard laughed. "A little hot, is it? That'll teach you to drag it to shade next time. Now get ahold of it and move!"

Ki stared at the iron bar at his feet. He knew that it would sear the palms of his hands if he grabbed it, so he did the only thing he could do and that was to relieve himself all over the pike. His piss actually steamed against the hot iron, and the guard started with surprise.

155

"Guess that must have cooled it down enough," Ki said, bending and retrieving the pike, then raising it and attacking the rock.

"Well, I'll be damned!" the guard swore as the other inmates chuckled. "I guess you're a smart one, ain't ya?"

Ki said nothing. He concentrated on the rock and getting it the hell out of the ground. That, and not passing out on his feet.

It was late afternoon when a lone rider appeared on the eastern horizon. Ki was still standing, but just barely. The pike seemed to weigh a hundred pounds, and every time he lifted it, an excruciating pain shot through his back and shoulders. The earth seemed to sway like a troubled ocean, and the road gang still had a good thirty yards to go before quitting time.

Jessie was also hot and a little faint. The intense heat coupled with the long hours she'd spent in the saddle were taking their toll. But she could see the outline of Yuma just ahead, and now she focused on the road gang.

Squinting her pretty green eyes and pulling her hat down lower on her forehead, Jessie stared at the guard and prisoners and wondered how anyone could be so inhumane as to work prisoners when the temperature was probably near 115 degrees.

And then she saw the samurai and her heart broke. "Ki!"

She whipped her horse into a run despite the heat and covered the last two miles in a rush. And because no one in his or her right mind would race a horse in such punishing heat, everyone stopped and stared at her.

The guards were so amazed to see that it was a pretty woman that they failed to think about stopping her, and then Jessie was leaping off her horse and grabbing the samurai.

The pike banged on the rocky road and tears glistened on Jessie's cheeks as she raised her head and shouted, "Who the hell is responsible for almost killing my poor husband! Which one of you!"

The guards and the prisoners gaped in amazement until finally the road gang boss managed to say, "Woman, that's a prisoner. I'm going to have to ask you to step away from him right now."

"Get me some water, you idiot!" Jessie cried, tearing off her hat and shading Ki's face before she leaned close and said, "I'm getting you out of there if I have to dynamite the walls tonight!"

"No," the samurai whispered. "Just get me off the pike for a few days."

Jessie was crying, and she nodded. "I'm so sorry."

"I'll be all right," Ki whispered in a voice that reflected his bone weariness. "And maybe, I might even find out who's behind everything."

Jessie desperately wanted to ask him to explain further, but that was impossible because the boss man came hurrying over with a dipper of water.

"You . . . you monster!" Jessie swore.

"Lady, I was just—"

"Get my husband in that wagon!"

"But we aren't finished for the day yet."

"*He* is!"

For a moment, the boss man tried to match Jessie's iron will, but he failed and turned to one of the guards. "Let's get this man back to the infirmary."

"No," Ki whispered, thinking of Big Al and how it would be impossible to protect himself. "My cell. Get me back to my cell."

"You heard him," Jessie said. "Who's your warden?"

"Warden Pitney, ma'am, but he don't brook no interference in the way that things are run around here."

Jessie allowed the guards to help Ki to the wagon. "How would he like to face charges of attempted murder?"

"What?"

"You heard me," Jessie said. "You were obviously trying to kill not only my husband, but all these prisoners, by working them in this horrible heat!"

The boss man rubbed his jaw. "It ain't no picnic for us guards either, ma'am."

Jessie marched back to her horse. "I'm going to see that there are some changes made."

"Well, who the hell are you?" a guard demanded.

"I'm someone that fights inhumanity and depravity when I see it practiced against man or beast."

Jessie said no more but instead mounted her horse and rode on toward Yuma. She knew that she had created all kinds of confusion. She had also arrived in the nick of time to help poor Ki. And as she rode on into town, she had to work not to start crying again, because in order to help the samurai, she had to be strong. Very, very strong indeed.

★

Chapter 17

That night, Elliot waited until their cellmates were asleep, then he dropped down beside the samurai's bunk and whispered, "I've got important news for you!"

"What kind?" Ki asked in a low voice.

"You were right about the judges being murdered. I heard from the trusty that works for Assistant Warden Haney that something is amiss."

Ki leaned closer to the man. "Be more specific."

"I can't," Elliot said. "I just know for sure that the assistant warden is up so something big and it has to do with that Richard Smith fella you mentioned. But it's so secret it's going to cost you a lot of money."

Ki was not a man to make false threats, and Elliot seemed to believe him when he said, "You will be very sorry if you are trying to trick me for money."

"I am telling you the truth!" Elliot croaked. "The assistant warden is up to something."

"But you don't know what?"

"Only that he hates Warden Pitney and wants his job. The

trustee who works for Haney swears that the man would do anything to become warden. Everyone in this pen stands to lose if that happens. Haney would reward a few trustees and work the rest of us to death."

"Is the warden appointed by the governor?"

"Yes, but he's nominated by . . . by the judges!"

"That's it then," Ki said with certainty. "It *has* to be."

"You mean that Haney is having the judges murdered just so that their replacements will nominate him as warden?"

"Exactly. But the corruption goes deeper than that," Ki said, "though I doubt if the governor himself is in on this plot. What we have is a corrupt judge—Potter—in failing health, who wants to name his replacement—Attorney Smith—who has found an over-ambitious assistant warden—Haney."

"So it's like a pyramid," Elliot said, with a shake of his head.

"That's right," Ki said. "Three rotten apples will spoil the whole barrel."

"But what can you do?" Elliot asked. "Why, you're certainly not in any position to cry wolf."

"Jessica can," Ki said.

Ki slipped a piece of wire out of his striped pants. "Then I guess that I'd better get Jessie some evidence to use against our assistant warden."

Elliot stepped back. "Do you really think you can pick the cell door lock with that?"

"I do and I will," Ki said, moving to the door, inserting the wire, and working it around and around.

"That won't do—"

"Shhh!" Ki ordered. "I need concentration."

Elliot backed up and leaned against the cell wall. He folded his arms across his chest and watched as Ki pressed

160

his cheek against the lock and worked the wire around and around, then in and out.

"I'm telling you, Ki, that won't do a damned thing. What you need is—"

The lock clicked open, cutting Elliot's advice off in mid-sentence. And when Ki eased the door open, Elliot whispered, "Well, I'll be damned!"

"Let's go," Ki whispered.

"What!"

"I said come along."

"Where?"

"To Haney's office, of course. We need to find some evidence."

"You're mad! In the first place, he wouldn't keep it out for anyone to find, and in the second place, his sleeping quarters are in the room right next to his office."

"All right," Ki said, closing the cell door but not locking it, "stay here."

"Wait!" Elliot ran up to the door. "Are you coming back?"

"Not if I find some evidence."

Haney gripped the cell door. "Listen," he pleaded, "I need to think this out for a couple of minutes."

"There's no time for that," Ki said, "but if I'm shot and killed, you need to tell Jessie exactly what you told me a few minutes ago. She'll know what to do, and she'll make it worth your time and trouble."

"This is crazy!"

Ki shrugged his shoulders and dropped into a crouch before he moved away, sticking to the shadows. He was *Ninja*, but he had no black, hooded *Ninja* costume. No matter. He would slip across the prison grounds and enter the assistant warden's office, and somehow, he would find evidence that Haney was involved in the death of Judge Appleton as well as other territorial judges.

Most likely, the assistant warden was using paroled convicts to do his bidding. The setup was a natural, and it would be easy to find ex-convicts willing to exchange an easy sentence for the pleasure of murdering a judge—perhaps even the very one that had sentenced them to prison.

Ki moved to the edge of the prison yard, and then he crouched in the shadows, his eyes fully adjusted to the darkness. In the moonlight, he could see the main prison tower with the big Lowell battery gun and the silhouette of a guard framed against the sky. Not fifty feet from where he crouched, a second guard silently patrolled the catwalk.

Ki fixed his attention on the assistant warden's office and sleeping quarters. It was about thirty yards away but directly across the exercise yard, where there was no cover.

The samurai watched the two guards for another ten minutes, until he was sure that he would not have a better opportunity; then he sprinted for Haney's office.

With his heart slamming against his ribs, Ki expected to feel a bullet tear through his lungs at any moment. The shot never came, and when he flattened against the adobe building, he knew that he was going to be all right until he attempted to make his escape.

A full minute passed before the samurai slipped into the assistant warden's office. He listened to Haney's snoring in the next room, then moved carefully across to the assistant warden's desk. It was locked and so were eight large file cabinets.

Ki took a deep breath. If he had been in possession of his *tanto* blade, he was sure that he could have opened all of them, but without a knife or key his job was going to be

162

much more difficult. The samurai had a choice to make, and he reached it swiftly. There simply was no time to open and pour through eight file cabinets. He needed evidence and he needed it in a hurry.

Ki pivoted toward the assistant warden's sleeping quarters. He moved catlike, and when he entered Haney's room, Ki wasted no time, but went directly to the man's bedside.

Placing his hand on the assistant warden's throat, he applied pressure until Haney's snoring suddenly degenerated into choking. Ki continuted to apply pressure, and Haney began to struggle as he grabbed the samurai's wrist and tried to pull it away.

But Ki's grip was as tight and unforgiving as the shackles that had chafed his ankle. The light was dim, but he could feel Haney's terror as he struggled for life-giving oxygen. Finally, Haney began to make terrible sounds deep in his throat, and that told Ki the man was close to death.

The samurai released his grip, and the assistant warden sucked in deep breaths. "Make a wrong move or try to yell, and all that will come out will be a croak. It will be the last sound you make."

It took the assistant warden several minutes before he regained his senses. By then Ki had searched the man's coat pockets and found a gun but no keys.

"I want you to unlock your desk and file cabinets," Ki said, placing the cold steel of a gun barrel against the man's forehead.

"What for?" Haney's voice was no more than a strangled whisper, which suited Ki just fine.

"You're behind the killing of Judge Stanley Appleton and the others. I want the proof to put you, Richard Smith, and Judge Potter away in this very prison."

"You can go to hell!"

Ki pistol-whipped the man across the bridge of his nose, breaking it with a sickening crunch. Haney cried out, and the samurai cocked back the hammer of his pistol and placed it right between the assistant warden's eyes.

Ki said, "I've got nothing to lose. Make your decision. The evidence, or your life."

With blood streaming down his face and neck, Haney's resolve broke. "All right! All right!"

Ten minutes later, Ki had his evidence, in the form of secret correspondence between the assistant warden, Richard Smith, and Judge Potter. Haney was slumped in his blood-stained nightshirt, holding a wet towel to his broken nose.

"Why did you keep these letters?" the samurai asked. "Just in case Smith or Potter failed their promises or tried to double-cross you?"

"Something like that."

Ki slipped the damning letters behind his waistband and stared at Haney with unconcealed dislike. "How many other judges besides Appleton?"

"Just two."

Ki shook his head. "*Just* two?" he challenged.

"Maybe three," Haney swore. "But I never killed any of them. Neither did Judge Potter or Richard Smith! They were killed by paroled convicts."

"I don't think the jury will find the convicts any less guilty than you, Judge Potter, or Richard Smith," Ki said. "Get up!"

"What are you going to do now?"

"We're going to see the warden."

Haney stood up. "If we go out into the yard, we'll be challenged. They might gun us down thinking we're trying to escape."

"Life is about taking chances," Ki said. "Let's go."

But Haney was suddenly afraid. "Listen," he pleaded, "let's wait until morning. The guards are under orders to open fire if they see something moving around out there."

"Then you'd better do some yelling or fast talking," Ki said, shoving the fat man toward the door. "That, or move fast and say your prayers."

Haney had to be pushed outside. Ki kept the assistant warden's body right in front of him as they crept toward the warden's office and living quarters.

"Help!" Haney screamed. "Help!"

Suddenly, the guard on the catwalk spun and covered them with his rifle. "Who goes there?"

Ki threw himself back into the shadows, but Haney broke away and raced forward. "It's . . . !"

The words were not completely out of the assistant warden's mouth when the guard fired. Ki saw Haney stagger, and then the tower guard opened fire, too. Ki was just fifteen feet away, and he saw the heavy bullets rip the assistant warden to pieces.

When Haney's corpulent body stopped kicking, the tower guard silenced his big gun and Warden Pitney exploded out of his office. "This is the warden, everyone hold your goddamn fire!"

The prison was alive with noise. Back in the rock cells, the inmates howled, and in the guards' barracks for single men, Ki could hear a great deal of shouting. Then he saw guards come pouring out with their rifles.

"Hold it!" Pitney shouted. "Everyone halt!"

A moment later, the warden was kneeling beside Haney. Throwing his head back, he shouted up at the tower and the catwalk guards, "You shot my assistant, damn you! This is Bill Haney!"

A guard swore to himself, but everyone else just stood rooted in stunned silence.

Warden Pitney stood up. "I want everyone to get a lantern and search every inch of this prison, and I want a cell count. Now!"

Ki pitched Haney's gun aside, then stepped out of the shadows. "That won't be necessary," he said. "I'm the only one loose."

The guards swung their rifles on the samurai, but this time, they held their fire.

"Raise your hands!" Pitney shouted.

Ki did as he was told. The guards rushed him and knocked him down. Several smashed their fists into Ki's face. "He's carrying . . . It's letters, Warden!"

"Bring him here!" the warden ordered.

Ki was dragged back to his feet and brought before the warden. "So, it's you. Well, I guess you've earned the gallows this time."

"Not quite," Ki said. "Read those letters."

The warden stared at him for a moment. "Bring him along," he said to the guards as he headed back to his office.

Minutes later, the warden slumped down in his chair, still dressed in his nightgown. "These letters will hang Smith and Judge Potter," he said. "Just as they'd have hanged Assistant Warden Haney."

"I think he understood that," Ki said. "That's why he gambled and lost outside."

"I'll send for the sheriff of Yuma immediately," the warden said. "The arrests will follow at once."

"I'd like to be released right now."

"I can't do that! You're a prisoner!"

"Sentenced by. . . ."

"Judge Potter," the warden said. "And sentenced before any of this was known. I'm sorry, but you'll be returned to your cell. In short order, there will be a formal inquiry, and at that time, perhaps your sentence will be commuted. But until then, I have no authority to release you."

"I'm sorry, too," Ki said, grabbing a rifle from one of the guards and turning it on the warden, "but I'm afraid that I can't wait."

"Nobody move!" Warden Pitney cried.

Ki was running a bluff, but it was his only hope. "You see, Judge Stanley Appleton was my friend. If I am locked up again, Richard Smith and Potter might get away clean. They're clever and resourceful men, and they have the money to disappear and never be found."

"It's a job for the marshal!"

"No," Ki told the warden, "it's a job for whoever can do it best. That's me and I'm leaving now."

The guards had their rifles trained on Ki until the warden said in a heavy voice, "Let him go."

"I want a horse. A good horse."

"Saddle my bay," the warden ordered one of his guards.

Ki waited until the man was outside, and then he said, "Warden, you're a good man and a fair one. I gave you those letters knowing the're all the evidence that's needed to hang or at least put Potter and Smith in prison for life."

"In a place like this, given their past, neither man would last a week."

"That's probably true," Ki said. "But unless you give me the chance to capture them before they escape, we'll never really know."

The warden steepled his fingers. "You're asking for time."

"That's right."

"I can't give you more than a few hours. That's all that I can stall. Any longer and I'll put my career in grave jeopardy."

"Daybreak," Ki said. "Give it until daybreak before you send for the marshal and the whole town hears about this."

Warden Pitney thought about that for almost a minute before he said, "There's few things I hate more than the thought of a corrupt judicial system. Apparently, that's what we have, and it would have gotten even worse if it were not for you."

"I'm not looking for praise," Ki said. "I just want out of Yuma Prison and a chance to nail Judge Potter and Attorney Smith before they smell danger and run."

"All right," Pitney said. "I'll give you that chance, though it might cost me my job."

"I don't think so," Ki said. "Not when all the chips have fallen."

"I hope you're right," Pitney said. "Now, will you get the hell out of my prison so I can get dressed and restore order?"

"Gladly."

"Guards," Warden Pitney said, "see that this . . . this . . ."

"Samurai," Ki told the man.

"Okay, samurai. See that he rides safely away on my horse."

The guards nodded, and though looking confused and apprehensive, they escorted Ki to the stable.

When the horse was ready, Ki started to mount but then remembered something.

"I came with my own clothes," he said. "I'd like to leave wearing them."

The guards exchanged glances, and the one who seemed to be in charge said, "We'll get them for you."

Several minutes later, Ki stripped out of his prison stripes and got back into his own, loose-fitting outfit.

"With your hair cut close, you still look like an escape," a guard commented.

"I guess so," Ki told them. "But when I next see Judge Potter and Attorney Smith, there will be no doubt in their minds who I am and why I returned."

Ki mounted his horse and turned it toward the open gate. The warden had taken a moment to slip into his pants and boots. He was stuffing his shirt in behind his belt when Ki reined his horse up.

"By the way," Ki said, "Haney's trusty bought their positions with bribes."

"I figured that."

"And another thing, one of the men in my cell, named Elliot, was a big help in getting information. I think you ought to make him a trustee and try to get him an early release, Warden."

"I'll put some hard thought to it," Pitney said.

"Good," the samurai replied as he wheeled his horse about and rode away.

When Ki passed back out through the heavy iron gates of the prison and took a deep breath of freedom, he sighed with joy. Now all he had to do was find Jessie, and together, they would bring Potter and Smith to a long overdue day of reckoning.

★

Chapter 18

Jessie had not asked the samurai any foolish questions the night he had awakened her in Yuma. She had simply dressed, grabbed her few belongings, and accompanied Ki to the stable to get her palomino horse before leaving.

The return trip across the Sonoran Desert had been hard, but uneventful. And now, as they rode down a low set of hills toward Tucson just as the sun was setting, Jessie and Ki knew that the long, hard trail was almost over.

"We've missed Austin in this desert," Jessie said. "He would have left for Yuma by now to help us."

"We won't need his help."

"I know, but I still hate to think of him riding all the way to Yuma to help us only to discover that we've already returned."

"It was a big desert," Ki said. "Right now, all I'm worried about is grabbing Attorney Smith before the man slips away."

"Without those letters you found in the assistant warden's office, we haven't any grounds to arrest either Judge Potter

170

or Smith," Jessie said. "So I guess we'll just have to play this one and let the cards fall as they will."

Jessie touched spurs to Sun's flanks, and the palomino galloped the rest of the way into Tucson. Jessie was well aware of the difficulties to be faced in the next hour or two, when they tried to apprehend Potter and Smith. Both men were wealthy, influential, and had many prominent friends. Arresting them would be difficult if not impossible without some proof to back their charges of murder, bribery, and extortion.

"Are you sure that Warden Pitney is honest and won't destroy those letters?" Jessie asked as they neared town.

"Absolutely."

"Then I think we ought to go see Rollin Adair before we do anything," Jessie said. "He can take a deposition before we move on Potter and Smith. That way, if something should happen to us, we've got everything on the record."

Ki nodded. When it came to fighting, he was the one that made the decisions, but when it came to matters of law, business, or finance, Jessie knew what was best.

"Ki, I'll go see Rollin at his hotel. You wait for me at Pearl's. Tell her what we know and that we might just need to hide at her place."

"I'd rather we stayed together," Ki said in one of the few times he'd ever voiced an objection.

"I know that, but I'm worried about Pearl and that death threat that she received."

Ki nodded and turned his horse away as they entered town in the late afternoon twilight. He was not at all pleased about letting Jessie go off to find Rollin Adair alone. He rode quickly to the Appleton house, and when he knocked on the door, Pearl's housekeeper and friend Mildred peered through the window, recognized the samurai, and opened the door in a rush of excitement.

"Ki! Thank heavens you're back! Something terrible has happened."

"What?"

"Pearl is missing!"

Ki placed his hands on the distraught woman's thin shoulders. "Just calm down," he said. "Tell me when she disappeared."

"About three days ago. That nice young man, Mr. Peter Austin, he just got out of jail and came by here that very same evening. They stayed up late talking in the judge's parlor, and I went to bed. But in the morning, they were both gone! I think he kidnapped her!"

Ki shook his head. "No. He wasn't that kind of a man. My guess is that someone must have gotten the drop on the both of them and taken them away."

"But where! And why?"

"I don't know. Probably for Pearl's money. I'd assume that the judge left her quite an inheritance. Mildred, Jessie says that she left some of my things in a bedroom. I think I need them now."

Mildred showed Ki where his things were. The samurai was more than happy to reclaim his extra *shuriken* star blades and his *tanto* knife. Going back outside, he said, "I'll return soon. Don't let anyone in except for that attorney, Rollin Adair. He should be along to protect you until Jessie and I get back."

"All right," Mildred promised. "But do you think they'd hurt Pearl?"

Ki, not wishing to alarm the poor woman any more than she was already, shook his head before he climbed back onto his horse. "Pearl is of no value to them dead. And so, if her money is still on deposit at the bank, it's almost certain that she's still alive. I wish I could feel the same way about Austin's chances."

Ki wasted no time in rejoining Jessie and Rollin Adair. Jessie, grim-faced, said, "Rollin told me about Pearl's disappearance. And of course, the sheriff is making a big show of trying to find them. He's sent his deputies out looking and so forth, but I think it's all an act."

Rollin Adair looked pale and upset. "I've been to Judge Potter, and I'm afraid I've threatened him without anything to back up my suspicions. He was furious. Swore he'd have me disbarred from the legal society so that I'd never be allowed to practice law again."

"The whole bunch are thicker than thieves," Jessie said.

"So what do we do first?" Ki asked.

Jessie thought a moment. "I say we need to get Judge Potter first. He's the weak link because of his drinking. I think he'll crack and tell us the truth if he's pressured hard enough."

Ki nodded, and Jessie started to go after him, but Adair said, "I want to come along."

"I think it would be better if you didn't," Jessie said. "That way, we've got someone who can help us if everything goes wrong."

Adair reluctantly nodded. "Do you think that Austin is in cahoots with the judge and Richard Smith?"

Jessie shook her head. "No. But I've misjudged men before, and I probably will again. We'll just have to wait and see. When we find Pearl, we'll find out about Austin."

"I wish there was something that I could do," the attorney said, pacing back and forth.

"There is. Write down everything I've told you about Assistant Warden Haney and this conspiracy to stack the court system with men like Richard Smith, then go watch over Mildred. But first, give me directions to Judge Potter's house."

Ki and Jessie left moments later. It was fully dark outside, and less than five minutes later, they turned the corner of a street and saw Judge Potter's home. It was a big Victorian house, two stories with lots of intricate woodwork, a beautiful porch, and a well-manicured yard.

Jessie frowned with disapproval. "I can see that the judge has done well for himself."

"He's probably been pocketing fines and taking bribes for most of his career," Ki said.

Jessie was sure that Ki was correct. The house before them would have cost a small fortune to build and maintain.

"If the judge or any of his men recognize you at his doorstep," Jessie said, "they're going to know something is drastically wrong. I think you had better ride around behind the house and wait there until I call."

"Just be careful," Ki said. "The judge is unstable and therefore very dangerous. He might be drunk and then panic the minute he sees you. He might also have a few 'friends' waiting inside."

"I'll be careful," Jessie promised, slipping a derringer out of her saddlebag and palming it in her left hand so that her right was still free to reach the Colt on her shapely hip.

Ki peeled away to ride around the block so that he could enter the judge's yard from the back alley while Jessie rode directly up to the hitching rail in front. She dismounted and tied her horse, then opened a picket fence gate and started toward the door and the big porch lantern that illuminated much of the walk.

"That's far enough, Miss Starbuck," a man said, stepping out of the shadows.

Jessie thought she recognized the man as Judge Potter's bailiff, but she could not be sure. "I came to see the judge."

"He's in bed for the night. Maybe you should come back in the morning."

"No," Jessie said. "I *must* see him right now."

"Sorry."

Jessie had not stopped walking, and when she was almost up to the man, she raised her left hand and cocked the hammer of the derringer back. "Inside," she ordered, "and don't make a sound."

The man's eyes bugged with outrage, but that cooled when he saw the determined look on Jessie's face. "You're making a big, big mistake, Miss Starbuck. Money or not, this will send you to prison just like it did your friend."

"That's my worry," Jessie said. "Now get inside."

When they were inside, Jessie closed the door behind her. "Where is he?"

The man shrugged. "Beats the hell out of me."

Jessie stepped forward and jammed the gun into the bailiff's soft stomach. "Where is he!"

"Upstairs! Third bedroom on the right."

"And where is Miss Appleton?"

"I don't know what the hell you're talking about," the man spat. Realizing that she could not leave this man alone for even a moment, Jessie said, "Let's go pay the judge a visit."

"Lady, you're making a big, big mistake."

"So are you if you don't shut up and do as I say," Jessie said, drawing her Colt so that she had a pistol in each hand.

175

They started climbing a beautifully hand-carved staircase and were halfway to the second floor when two men burst out of an upstairs bedroom and saw Jessie.

"Hey!" one yelled. "what the . . ."

The bailiff shouted a warning and threw himself over the side of the stairs, crashing off a big table below as the two men upstairs drew their guns.

Jessie shot one in the chest, but the other fired a bullet that made her jump backward and almost tumble down the stairs. When she caught her balance, she unleashed two more shots from her Colt, driving the man back into a bedroom.

Dazed, Jessie started back up the stairs, but Ki flew past her, and when he reached the second landing, he hurled himself at the bedroom door, smashing it open and driving the gunman behind it to the floor.

Jessie reached the landing in time to see the man attempt to lift his gun, but Ki's foot came up in a sweep lotus and connected just under the man's jaw. There was a sickening crack of bone, and Jessie saw the gunman quiver in death.

"Pearl!" Jessie cried, rushing into the bedroom.

"Damn you!" a voice hissed from behind.

Jessie half turned, and she saw Judge Potter with a gun in his boney fist. Potter raised the weapon and fired, but Ki was already driving forward in a low dive. He struck Potter at the knees and, together, they crashed through the railing and dropped to the floor below.

"Ki!" Jessie shouted, leaving Pearl to race back down to the samurai. "Ki, are you all right!"

The samurai was dazed but unhurt. "I landed on top," he said, climbing a little unsteadily to his feet. "But the judge didn't fare so well."

Jessie knelt and placed her fingertips against the judge's carotid artery. "He's dead."

"But Pearl is alive," Jessie said, leaving her samurai to hurry back upstairs. She tore the gag from Pearl's mouth. "Are you all right?"

"Yes," she sobbed, "but they may have killed Austin!"

Jessie's heart sank. "Are you sure?"

"No," Pearl said, tears leaking out of her eyes. "We were in my father's library when it happened. After they knocked Austin to the floor, they took his body away and brought me here."

"Did you see Richard Smith in the judge's house at any time ?"

"No," Pearl said, "but I heard his voice downstairs. Once, he was yelling at the judge, and I thought they were going to kill each other, they sounded so angry."

"I wish they would have," Jessie said.

Jessie finished untying Pearl and helped her to her feet. "Are you able to walk? Here, put your arm over my shoulder and let's get out of here before people start showing up after hearing the gunfire."

Jessie helped Pearl downstairs as fast as she could. "Is the bailiff still alive?"

Ki was kneeling over the man. "Yes. But he's badly shaken."

"Bring him along," Jessie said. "We're going to need his testimony."

Ki nodded and threw the bailiff over his shoulder. A few minutes later, they were moving out the back door and down the dark alley, leading Ki's horse. Jessie would return for her own horse later.

They reached Pearl's house, and Mildred threw herself into Pearl's arms, sobbing with happiness.

Ki said, "Please, Jessie, allow me to take care of Richard Smith alone."

Jessie nodded her assent, knowing that this was a situation where the samurai would actually be hampered by her presence. "Try to take him alive."

The samurai nodded and slipped out the doorway. He moved silently through the dark streets until he came to Smith's own fine home. The lights were on, and through the curtains, Ki could see the silhouettes of two men inside.

He hopped over the back fence and moved silently to the front door. He could hear the voices distinctly now, and it sounded as if they were arguing.

"I say we need to kill him!" Smith hissed. "What good is he to us now!"

"I don't know, but all of this is finished now. We've got to get out of town this very minute!"

Ki's heart sank. There was no mistaking the voice of a very excited Rollin Adair. It suddenly occurred to Ki that Adair had never worked a "deal" with Judge Potter in order to get him a light jail sentence. Adair had been in on this from the start. Oh, he had befriended Pearl and made it seem that he was Judge Potter's enemy, but that had been a well-conceived ruse. Ki would not have been surprised if Adair had had designs on Pearl's inheritance from the beginning.

The samurai crouched low and moved over to the front door. Turning the handle, he opened the door while slipping a *shuriken* star blade from his pocket.

"The game is up," he said to the two startled attorneys.

Adair paled. Richard Smith acted. The attorney reached for a gun, and Ki waited a split second before he hurled the star blade, hitting Smith in the forearm.

"Ahhh!" the attorney cried.

Rollin Adair bolted for the hallway, but Ki anticipated this and pounced on the frightened man. One chopping blow to the base of Adair's neck caused him to collapse into unconsciousness.

Ki hurried back down the hallway just in time to see Smith scooping up the gun he'd dropped.

Ki took his last star blade from his pocket. "Don't do it," he warned.

Smith hesitated. The man's eyes burned with hatred. "You'll never bring me to trial. This whole thing will blow up in your face and you'll hang!"

"Let's find out," Ki said in a quiet voice.

"Judge Potter will make you regret the very day you were born."

"He's dead," Ki said. "And Pearl is safe. She'll testify to everything."

"She can't *prove* anything!"

"She saw you at the judge's house, where she was being held hostage."

"That's a lie!"

It was a lie, but Ki's face didn't betray him. "She scooted her chair to that upstairs bedroom door and managed to look downstairs. And Adair will testify, too. He's going to try and save his own skin. You're finished."

In a fit of desperate rage, Smith grabbed the pistol with his left hand and attempted to thumb back the hammer. His movement was very slow and clumsy because his right arm was bleeding profusely.

"Don't!" Ki shouted.

But Smith wasn't listening. He finally managed to get the hammer back, and with the gun barrel shaking violently, he tried to take deadly aim at the samurai.

Ki's arm whipped forward, and the *shuriken* blade spun

wickedly across the room. Ki watched as his star blade embedded itself in Smith's forehead and brought the attorney crashing to the floor.

The samurai walked over the dead man to grab a bottle of liquor. He returned to the hallway and rolled Adair over on his back, then poured the liquor over the unconscious attorney's face.

"Wake up!" he ordered, slapping Adair until he regained consciousness. "Where is Austin James?"

"Downstairs, tied up in the basement," Adair said groggily. "He's still alive. We were just keeping him in case we needed him to get Pearl's money!"

"Get up," Ki ordered, dragging Adair to his feet. "Let's go get Austin. Maybe I'll just let him even the score with you."

"Please," Adair said. "You've got to understand that none of this was my idea. But I was starving and—"

"Shut up," Ki said. "You can tell it all to an honest judge—if there are any left in the Arizona Territory."

Two weeks later, Jessie and Ki tied their horses to the back of a Concord stage and bid farewell to Austin, Pearl, and a tearful Mildred.

"You come visit," Jessie said, "all of you."

Pearl took Austin's arm and hugged it tightly. "Will you come to our wedding?"

Jessie had to be honest. She had seen enough of Arizona to last her a good long while. "No," she said truthfully. "I have a cattle ranch to run and a lot of business to take care of. But perhaps I'll send Ki in my place."

The samurai groaned. "I think I had also better remain in Texas and try to be the father that little Ricardo has always wanted and needed."

Jessie's teasing smile evaporated. After coming to realize that his real father was no good, a dejected Ricardo had departed Tucson on the previous stage, to return to his mother's side.

"We'll see that Ricardo, his mother, and his sister have a much better life at Circle Star than they've had in Juárez," Jessie vowed.

Ki very much looked forward to seeing the young Mexican boy who reminded him so much of his own tragic and fatherless childhood. He would teach Ricardo many things, as would Jessie's vaqueros. And someday, the boy of two races would grow up to be a strong and good man. One that his father, Richard Smith, would have envied, if he had lived to spend the rest of his days in the Yuma Prison.

Watch for

**LONE STAR AND
THE OKLAHOMA RUSTLERS**

110th novel in the exciting LONE STAR series
from Jove

Coming in October!

WESTERNS!

at least a savings of $3.00 each month below the publishers price. Second, there is never any shipping, handling or other hidden charges—Free home delivery. What's more there is no minimum number of books you must buy, you may return any selection for full credit and you can cancel your subscription at any time. A TRUE VALUE!

Mail the coupon below

To start your subscription and receive 2 FREE WESTERNS, fill out the coupon below and mail it today. We'll send your first shipment which includes 2 FREE BOOKS as soon as we receive it.

Mail To: 10670
True Value Home Subscription Services, Inc.
P.O. Box 5235
120 Brighton Road
Clifton, New Jersey 07015-5235

YES! I want to start receiving the very best Westerns being published today. Send me my first shipment of 6 Westerns for me to preview FREE for 10 days. If I decide to keep them, I'll pay for just 4 of the books at the low subscriber price of $2.45 each; a total of $9.80 (a $17.70 value). Then each month I'll receive the 6 newest and best Westerns to preview Free for 10 days. If I'm not satisfied I may return them within 10 days and owe nothing. Otherwise I'll be billed at the special low subscriber rate of $2.45 each; a total of $14.70 (at least a $17.70 value) and save $3.00 off the publishers price. There are never any shipping, handling or other hidden charges. I understand I am under no obligation to purchase any number of books and I can cancel my subscription at any time, no questions asked. In any case the 2 FREE books are mine to keep.

Name _____

Address _____ Apt. # _____

City _____ State _____ Zip _____

Telephone # _____

Signature _____
(if under 18 parent or guardian must sign)
Terms and prices subject to change.
Orders subject to acceptance by True Value Home Subscription Services, Inc.